FUCK HAPPINESS

KIRK JONES

ATLATL

Atlatl Press
POB 521
Dayton, Ohio 45401
atlatlpress.com

This one is for John Perrault, the baddest ass bad asser that ever bad assed an English 12 classroom.

How you put up with two generations of the Jones family is beyond me.

Thanks for the tough love, teach.

FUCK HAPPINESS

FOREWORD

AS I grew into adolescence during the much too short age of the Kennedy presidency, many of us adopted the Biblical "'Tis better to light a candle than to curse the darkness" as our mantra. We believed strongly that our job in life was to do well and to do good.

Even in the face of increasing adversity our world offers up, that belief persists today. You'll find it here, and in all of Kirk's work. If you're a rookie reader of his books, welcome to this marvelous world of wonder. If you're a voracious veteran of his work as I am, welcome back. All Jones' writings capture the vagaries of life through a splendidly bizarre new lens. It is a dazzling combination of angst and humor in which hope always manages to make it out alive in some form or another.

We can only hope that his practice of lighting literary candles will continue. We desperately need them.

Thank you, my friend.

John R. Perrault

ONE
SHIT AND STARDUST

THE average human fecal deposit is roughly 3.5 ounces.

The world population is fast approaching 7 billion.

Assuming that a bowel movement occurs at least every three days—given natural homeostatic function—humans are producing 24.5 billion ounces of shit on a weekly basis.

Around 1.5 billion pounds of shit on a weekly basis.

Given these figures, it is inevitable that someday—cosmic years from now—the human race will keep growing and eventually produce waste equivalent to the weight of the planet. On that day, the shit that breaks mother earth's back will tilt her off her axis and hopefully launch our shit-soaked sphere toward the sun.

Our remains will become galactic confetti, shit and stardust supernova party favors.

In the grand scheme of things, you imagine this is inconsequential . . . everything is shit.

But you take solace in the fact that, at some point in history—before everything sprang into being—there was a time void of waste. Something prefigured the cosmic dump that snowballed into what the universe has become today.

You wonder what that something ate.

FUCK HAPPINESS

You realize you are hungry.

You wish information nourished you more. You consume it, but it never fills you. It simply runs through you, or escapes your ethereal orifices like heat from a poorly insulated home. Somewhere on the outskirts of your body, you imagine there's an auric colostomy bag of information hanging near one of your chakras, ready to burst. Ready to infect you if it isn't emptied soon.

Information is a parasite that selectively harms its hosts.

Most people are lucky. They share a symbiotic relationship with their parasite.

You're not so lucky. Information eats away at your insides. It perverts reality, attempts to supplement your paranoid delusions with sensory input. When you worry your wife's fucking another man, you actually see it. You can taste her in the moment. Her sex tastes like sweat and rejection. Her asshole smells like bleach and calcium carbonate.

In this false memory, the dirtiest part of her body smells like cleaning agents, and that is the only part of the memory that lets you know something is off.

Your false memory folds in on reality, and you're remembering her fucking someone else while you smell her asshole.

Part of you knows your wife never cheated on you. Part of you believes it is currently happening. These two realities paradoxically coexist inside you.

You remember that scene in *Event Horizon* where Dr. Weir explains wormholes. He folds a piece of paper in half and slides the pencil through, connecting two different points in time. What you're experiencing is a bit like this, except with information. Your mind travels on threads of data, some real, some birthed by your imagination. Somewhere along the line, reality and fantasy cross threads, and certain parts of the mind can make neither heads nor tails of it.

You stop yourself, afraid your nightmare might somehow become a reality.

You wish you could expel the information, shit it out like a cosmic dump. But if you could, the information might infect others.

You've thought about this for a long time. You know all information is infectious. Every idea is a new disease, so you weave small bytes of information together in non-sequitur patterns, creating data strain vaccines.

You sit in the middle of your floor with a stack of VHS cassettes, clipping short pieces from the tapes within and scotching them together. Small clips from your childhood spliced with video from your wedding and public domain cartoons from the '30s protect you from memories your loved ones try to share with you. PBS poetry documentaries coupled with holocaust footage protects you from the violence of intellect.

So far, your vaccines have been highly personalized. But you know if you want to save the world, you have to transfer these data strains, unfiltered, to the masses.

You tried. You wrote your M.A. thesis in data strain. You turned in the first chapter: thirty pages of words in magazine clippings and blackout poetry filtered through a computational linguistics program and reorganized by prominence.

They escorted you off campus three days later and confiscated your hard drive.

Your wife—bless her soul—stuck around for another year.

Then you started speaking in data strain so the kids wouldn't get infected with your disease.

She left.

You still speak in data strain sometimes, and you're dabbling in visual data strains now. You've been renting VHS tapes from Giga Video down the road, cutting the tape into fragments, splicing clips from other VHS tapes in, and returning them.

You steer clear of the new releases. Right now you just need a small test group, so you go for cult classics, cutting short passages from the tape and inserting non-sequitur clips from your own collection taped together.

If you only wanted to save yourself, you could stay silent and withdraw completely from the world. But communication is a compulsion.

So to prevent people from getting infected when you speak to them you rely on sequence randomizers, paraphrase tools. You translate your writing to Japanese, then Portuguese, then back to English. You do whatever you can so the most dangerous diseases coming out of your head get out of your head but are untranslatable, unintelligible to others. You have to purge yourself of your thoughts, but you have to pasteurize them, make sure they aren't infectious.

It's horticulture of the mind. To reap the repercussions, for percussion to recede a roll of reaping. Green grasps the brass manifold movements, wrought stable relative reality. Relative stable reality wrought.

That is the only way.

You wake each morning before the alarm goes off, generally to a knock at the door.

Today a sheet is draped over the broken curtain rod, but the light always gets in. So you hang a ratty sleeping bag over the curtain rod until the rod begins to bend under the weight of everything suspended from it. You remind yourself you need to replace it. You think it just like that: *You need to replace that fucking curtain rod, Milton.* But you still don't know why you don't think of yourself in the context of *I* or *me.* You're not sure if your go-to self-reference is *you* because attaching *I* to everything in your life is too painful or because you've detached a part of yourself from the whole, a part that doesn't refer to itself in any person because it only exists to distance you from yourself and keep you in line . . . probably also because your life is so goddamned shameful that even your own brain can't stand to be a part of it.

You don't even know what part of "I" would be you anyway.

You brush your teeth and decide that's the last time you're going to think about it.

Someone knocks at the door.

It's your wife, Beth.

Your ex-wife, Beth.

You open the door and wipe the Colgate foam from the edges of your lips. "Hi, Beth."

"Hi, Milton. How's that chapbook coming along?"

"Actually—"

She jams her foot in the door defensively, like you're going to slam it in her face. "—Don't care. Child support. You're going to lose your fucking license."

You run to the kitchenette counter and dig through your wallet. "I think I have something in my bank account."

She scoffs. "You're just saying that to stay on my good side, hoping I'll fuck you. Not. Happening."

She's right.

When your ex left, she cut you off completely. She won't let you touch her. You've been orbiting her body ever since, trying to get back inside her. It took two weeks to learn that, even though she won't let you touch her, she'll touch you if you let her. But the touch can't be romantic or sexual in nature. It has to be flesh on flesh with no connotation of intimacy.

Two weeks after she left, you told her you thought you had lice, and that she'd need to check your head before she dropped the kids off. She ran her hands through your scalp, and you remembered the way those delicate fingers felt on other parts of your body. You remembered the way she used to run her hands through your chest hair and smile up at you.

The day she checked you for lice she lurched over your head with a cigarette in one hand and a tuft of your hair in the other. "You're clear."

You turned to her, almost catching the cigarette with your ear. "You sure?"

She pushed your head lightly. "I'm not going to stroke your scalp until you bust a nut, pervert."

You wanted to ask her for a blowjob, but you'd been drinking for weeks and your crotch smelled like wet dog. Still does. You sweat constantly since she left. So instead you waited a few weeks and told her your lower back hurt. Knowing already she wasn't going to give you a rub down, you asked her to lightly step on your back with her marathon shoes. To your surprise, she agreed.

She came over before the kids were home from school, laced up her Hoka One Ones, and asked, "How we doing this?"

You lay on the floor and she stepped up onto your lower back, just like she used to step up on the scale when she took up running.

You felt the soles of her shoes squish into the fat coalescing around your spine. "Just a little harder," you said, trying to sound objective and emotionally void.

She stomped your lower vertebrae with the heel of her shoe. "Like that?"

This felt right. You were working together. "That's perfect."

She heard it in your voice. You were happy. That was a mistake.

She stopped. "I better head out. Kids will be home soon."

That night you finally allowed yourself to think about her again while you touched yourself. You allowed yourself to hope.

Today she's already onto you. She knows you're beginning to sexualize non-sexual physical contact. "I'm not doing your back again." She takes a drag off her cigarette. "I feel like you violated my feet."

You kneel in front of your VCR and eject your last project. "I just asked you to step on my back for a minute. I didn't even get an erection."

"Don't talk about erections. Christ, Milton. If you keep talking like that we're going to have to keep these conversations in print so I can document them."

"I was just saying." You slip the cassette into its shit brown hard shell case. "It's a platonic thing, you know? I don't mean anything by it."

"It doesn't matter what you see it like or intend. If I feel like you raped my feet, don't minimize it."

"You're right. I'm sorry."

She takes another drag off her cigarette, sighs. "I guess I could bring over my shoes if you want."

While she bargains with you, you throw on a neon yellow hoodie and an old pair of soft-sole shoes. "I don't know . . ."

"Fucking mind games. I want my money."

You cradle your Giga Video late return and head for the door. "Be right back."

You walk across the road to take a twenty out of the Giga Video ATM. Gary, the cashier, looks up from the front desk and waves when you walk through the front door. "How's it going, Milton?"

"Not bad." You throw your late return on the counter and follow Gary's eyes to his sketch pad. "What you working on?"

"I'm getting better at adults. Figured I'd try my hand at kids for a while."

You watch him pencil a toddler's face with uncanny clarity. "I'd say you've got kids down too."

"Thanks, man."

Gary's alright. He knows your dirt. He knows, and he doesn't judge.

You used to go to college together. He wasn't there the day they tore you out of your seat in Dr. Washburn's class, but you see sympathy in his eyes.

Small town. Everybody knows. Everyone's infected. The bloated bald fuck browsing new release posters out front—on some level—knows.

The store manager chain-vaping apple-scented tar knows.

They all look at you with a combination of pity, fear, and hate.

Except Gary. His eyes exude only pity.

You shuffle to the ATM machine near the romantic comedies.

"Child support?" he asks.

"I'm hoping there's enough in there."

Gary closes his sketch pad and wipes the counter down with a week-old rag. "You going out this weekend? There's a transfer kid you should meet."

"Oh yeah?" The ATM asks if you want to check your balance first. You do not. If there isn't twenty, you just want the machine to tell you "insufficient funds" so you can get the fuck out of here.

"He wants to talk to you about your thesis."

The ATM prompts you to select your account. You select checking. The concept of savings is completely alien to you. "Where'd he hear about that?"

Gary looks down. "I told him."

You enter your pin number. You should have never told Gary. He's probably infected now.

"You should come out."

"Maybe next weekend. Hoping I'll have the kids tonight."

"Must be a trip, being a dad."

"Yeah." The machine dispenses twenty dollars. Then the ATM shows you your balance, even though you asked it not to. $1.49. Yeah . . . having kids is a real trip. Twelve trips to the fucking fridge after each meal because the nitrate-filled hot dog chunks were only fit for grinding into the carpet with their feet while they coated their DVDs with mac and cheese fingerprints. Six trips to the emergency room in one year after your mother bought them a used trampoline with broken netting. "A trip right to the fucking psych center, at the rate things are going."

"I think I'd like it."

"Give it a shot. Finish college first though, if you can." You head for the door.

"Wait a second!" Gary pulls a hard shell case from below the counter and slides it to your side.

You turn back.

"It's a weird one. Right up your alley. Check it out."

You open the case. It's a copy of *Country Cuzzins*. "Horror?" you ask.

Gary shakes his head. "Softcore porn meets *Hee Haw*."

"Right up my alley, eh?"

Gary laughs. "Just check it out, man."

You tuck it under your arm. "Alright. I better get back. Beth's waiting."

He sighs. "Alright. Later!"

When you get home Beth is standing near her bile green boat in the driveway.

You hand her a wadded up twenty. "It's all I have."

She fists the dollop of daddy dollars that'll dance their way to the marijuana dispensary down the road. "I'll use it to buy Karen a few pairs of pants."

"Sure you will."

She reaches into the back pocket of her jean shorts and pulls out a pack of Camel Wides. "You want one?"

You look into the back seat of the car. Your kids, Karen and Tommy, watch you intently. "I shouldn't."

She slaps the pack on her thigh, pulls one out. "They won't judge."

"It doesn't feel right."

"You know what doesn't feel right?" She kicks at the gravel below your feet. "Not knowing when you'll finally start pitching in with the kids."

"What doesn't feel right is not being able to see my kids."

"I'll let you take them for the weekend." She grabs you by the arm and pulls you to the doorway. "I want to talk to you first."

You glance one last time at the car before she pulls you onto the front porch, slams the door, and kisses you.

A drape of flies buzz against the door window.

You pull away. "What was that for?"

"I haven't fucked anyone since you left."

"I haven't either."

She starts to unbutton your pants. "Not that I wouldn't. I just haven't had the chance."

"Thanks?"

She pulls down your pants and takes your member into her hand. You're half hard already. She looks up at you.

The flies begin to settle. Light weaving through small gaps in their colony strobes slowly across your body.

She pauses.

She throws your dick against your balls. "Did you actually think that was going to happen?"

You put yourself away and zip up your pants. "What the fuck?"

The flies smash their heads repeatedly against the glass. The resulting drone sounds like electric laughter.

She drops her cigarette on the concrete and stomps it before even lighting it. "Fuck you."

"Why are you being like this? *You* left *me*!"

"I didn't have a choice." She stares up at you. "The shit you had laying around made 'all work and no play makes Jack a dull boy' look like a fucking copy of *See Spot Run*." Her spiked hair tickles your chin.

"I'm sorry," you tell her. "Will you please let me fuck you?"

She puts her hands on her hips. "Beg."

"Like, on my knees?"

"Good idea. Yes. On your knees."

The flies' white noise chortles continue.

You reluctantly lower yourself to the concrete, dusting away Beth's cigarette butt.

She unzips her pants and pulls them down to her lower thighs. She takes down her panties. Her bush is unkempt.

"You're so beautiful," you say. You run your hands down her thighs.

She drives your face into her pussy. She leans back so her pubic bone bears down on your nose. Is she trying to suffocate you?

You can still breathe. You know this because she smells like her cunt has been smoking blunts.

She smokes so much green weed her pussy smells like a Christmas tree.

You feel yourself begin to climax. You try to hang onto the moment, but you feel your consciousness slipping.

Every. Fucking. Time. Every time you have an orgasm since your wife left, your mind completely shuts down.

Sometimes you just go blank. You become unthinking as all faculties shift to your tactile reality. Sometimes even your sense of touch cuts off. You feel nothing.

Sometimes you're transported to a memory from earlier in life completely unrelated to sex. You think this is the brain's revenge on your body for giving you a boner in seventh grade math class.

Those non-sequitur masturbatory transitions are always the most unsettling. One minute you're trying to breathe through a thick mat of pine-scented pubic hair. The next you're sitting at the blood pressure machine in Kinney Drugs. An alarm sounds just before your reading appears on screen. You're 28 and you have hypertension. Then some part of your mind activates, reminding you, *Hey. You're sniffing pussy, dipshit. You shouldn't be doing this in public.* And it takes a minute for the rest of your brain to catch up, to realize you're not actually inhaling blue spruce cunt at the blood pressure machine. You're in the safety of your apartment—or at least the porch of your apartment—huddled down in the gravel. That's when you realize The Beatles were wrong. Happiness isn't a warm gun. Happiness is the spontaneous manifestation of a shame and sex-infused scenario—a group of pharmacy techs watching you inhale your ex-wife at the local drug store—and the subsequent sense of relief that washes over you when you open your eyes and realize you're cradled in your ex-wife's labia and no one is watching but her.

Beth pushes you away. "That's it."

"Don't leave me hanging like this."

She points to the load in your pants. "I'd barely call that hanging."

You look down. The throbbing in your abdomen and lower back tells you that you came.

You never felt it.

Beth pulls another cigarette out of her pocket. "Go clean up. I'll give you ten minutes. Then I'm sending the kids in."

You rush upstairs to your second-floor apartment, down the short hallway to your front door, and change into your college sweats. Before you have both legs in, you hear the kids running up the stairs. You're elated, but you just need to get your feet through these fucking holes so they don't burst through the door while your pants are around your ankles.

Tommy is first through the door. He throws his plastic bag of clothes in the corner and plops down on the couch. Karen runs up to give you a hug. Her hair is pulled tight in some sort of cross-woven series of braids. It's going to be a bitch to comb out after bath night tomorrow, which is likely why Beth did it.

"Missed you, Daddy."

"I missed you too." You pull her into your belly and smell her hair: ozone and synthetic berries.

You imagine this is likely the smell of stardust.

You imagine you're probably wrong, just like you were wrong about pussy smelling like cinnamon when you were seven.

But there's one thing you are sure of. These kids are the closest thing to purity—to 'not shit'—in the universe.

You head for the kitchenette. "You guys want something to eat? I have some hot dogs in the fridge."

TWO
HAPPINESS IS STAGNATION

W HEN you were old enough to have ideals and young enough to afford them, you hated Super Center. Your economics professor told you they were the new monopoly. Companies couldn't buy up the entire market for a single product anymore. So corporations instead bought up massive shares of every market. They did everything. Since the day you first heard that in 1999, the local Super Center has expanded to include an automotive garage, an optometrist, and a pharmacy. In some states the cocksuckers even perform minor surgeries just a few self-checkout lanes from the Pokémon cards.

Now you love Super Center. Politics be damned.

Your favorite part of any weekend is walking through those automated doors. You love being greeted by the aging man with a diaper bulge that makes you feel young enough to afford ideals again. Except you've been broken down by reality to the degree that you decide not to purchase.

Scratch that. You know better than to purchase, because there's no warranty plan on ideals. And the fuckers always bend and break.

Once you get past that first row of security panels, the kids dart away from you toward the seasonal aisles in the front. You linger on the clothes and magazines, watching your children from the corner of your eye. This is relative solitude. This is the modern equivalent of children being seen and not heard.

In a society where nearly everything is automated, Super Center is your semi-daycare. Take the little shits to the video game aisle. Let them smash the buttons on snot-soaked controllers while they scream at a frozen screen. You browse the games from the latest system, even though you haven't enjoyed a game since the 16-bit era.

Street Fighter is still kicking around. How about that?

Take them to the toy section, let your son's plastic pro wrestlers chase cardboard-encased supermodel facsimiles up and down the aisles. You listen from the neighboring fitness aisle, contemplate buying the same fucking barbell set and, again, decide it is too much.

Take them to dental care. Let them press the new sound-emitting toothbrushes against their temples to see if they can recognize the inappropriate pop song radiating through their tiny skulls. You smell deodorant until your allergies flare up. Remember you need to buy more cetirizine. So you can wear deodorant without sneezing every five minutes. So you don't smell when you talk to women. So you can have more children and spend more fucking time in the deodorant aisle.

You wouldn't have it any other way.

Super Center is your key to half happiness. Anything more is suicide.

Your children beat at your ankles with discount pool noodles. Winter is almost here. It reminds you of the first time you were truly happy. Her name was Spring. You dated her your first semester in college. She went down on you after Algebra every day for three weeks before you finally asked her to be your girlfriend. But the way she smiled . . . that was what really made you happy.

She smiled.

You smiled.

She read your poetry.

You smiled.

She smiled.

You fucked her.

She beat you with pool noodles.

You gained twenty-five pounds.

She failed out of Algebra.

You gained weight until the rolls on your stomach smiled back at you when you sat down. You gained weight until your cock buried itself, threatening to never come back.

She left.

You grew despondent.

You lost forty pounds and then some.

Home rings, a cat-gut string overture in the overturned stomach.

You became boisterous. You wrote poems. You recited drunken poetry outside of the residence halls.

Misery set your soul on fire, and it consumed the world around it. It burned bright like a beacon, drawing pussy to you like a moth to the flame.

Then you found Beth or Beth found you. And you were happy again.

But she never smiled.

You wrote your last poem the night before you asked her to marry you.

Poetry was your dowsing rod, your compass on the road to happiness. Once you found what you thought you were looking for, the function of writing was lost.

This is a pattern repeating itself throughout all of human existence. Desire and longing are inspiration. The muse is and should remain unattainable. To satiate is to die. Happiness is stagnation. Think of all the miserable fucks throughout history whose names have become timeless:

Charles Schulz was allegedly beaten by peers with corncobs, neglected by his mother, and loathed the memory of his childhood.

His hatred fueled a successful career well into his twilight years.

Ernest Hemingway was allegedly dressed as a baby girl, married and divorced several times, was a raging alcoholic, and ended up committing suicide in a world he frequently felt alienated from.

He was one of the most successful writers in American history.

Jonathan Swift was a misanthropist who reveled in pissing the general population off. He suggested the rich eat babies to solve the crisis of poverty, a proposal that disgusts readers incapable of processing satire to this day.

To. This. Day.

Those names are just off the top of your head.

Your children continue to beat your ankles. The noodles tear at your flesh until your shins are raw. Tommy takes the noodle and rubs it back and forth across your leg. You think you smell burning hair. You want to scream. You want to tell them to stop.

But a small fire—rendered from skinflint kindling and a small spark of pain—burns at your feet.

The stock boy looks up from the Hot Wheels display he's toiling away at.

He smells it. He senses it.

His name is Bob. You know this because his nametag reads "Bob."

He smiles.

You smile.

Flaring opaque, vivid invisible blackness smeared light through the intangible composite, like a photonegative.

THREE
CHAMBER FLIES AND
BITCH TITS

HAPPINESS (*'hæpinəs*) *n.* **1.** a dark room in a quiet part of New York where the night's silence is only occasionally punctuated by squealing tires and gunshots. The convenience store and adjoining video rental store's a block down. The fluorescent lighting barely makes its way past the neighboring building and through your curtains. The faint red glow of your digital alarm clock cascades across your IKEA nightstand like a rising tide onto the sand in your eyes **2.** as you touch yourself, you never go soft thinking about the girls who told you to meet them with your pants down in the Monopole bathroom, the ones who charged in, blinded you with their cameras, and ran. You don't think about the trail of hair climbing up the sides of your shaft, earning you the nick name "Burnsie" in high school.

. . . and you're soft again.

You clap on the light in your bedroom and dig for the remote to turn the TV on. *Married with Children* whispers in hushed tones to you. The laugh track is louder than the dialogue.

It reminds you of home. When-you-were-a-child home. You always loved the show. Despite the fact that the Bundys somehow lived in what seemed to be the good part of town—nice house, friendly neighbors—they represented the lowest acceptable denominator. Even though they had nothing, they still took pleasure in the luxuries only American poverty can afford. Even though Al Bundy hated his life most days, he still found pleasure in cold beer, tits, and misogyny.

You, on the other hand, haven't drank in months, haven't touched a pair of tits in weeks, and the humanities helped beat the misogyny out of you years ago. Most of it, anyway.

But you still have television. You still have the late-night infomercials and syndicated fantasies that are just close enough to your reality to seem "in touch" and just far away enough to allow escape.

You're too tired tonight, however. The kids took the piss out of you at Super Center. You're ready for that digital tidal wave of red to cascade across your nightstand, over the divots in your pillow, and into the cave of blankets you bury yourself in. You're ready to sink into your happy place. Your "me" place.

Strangely, though the cluttered middle-class residences of sitcom families resonate with you, your happy place is a one-room cabin in the woods. There's a cot, a fireplace, and a small desk filled with your poetry. There's an inkwell, even though you prefer typing. But you're never writing when you imagine it. You're always doing the same fucking thing you are when you finally have time to think about your dream life: lying down to go to sleep.

So you lie in bed dozing off, fantasizing about lying in bed dozing off somewhere else. You fantasize about a smaller living space after wondering where your kids are going to sleep because your apartment is too small. You fantasize about owning less shit after a day of accumulating more shit at Super Center.

You dream Al Bundy is your research partner. You're conducting a corpus linguistics study on bitch tits. Bundy tells you to go long for an algorithm pass. You fumble. The ball changes hands.

"Bitch tits," you whisper to yourself. By this you mean your tits are bigger than your ex-wife's tits.

"Bitch tits," the pair of bitch tits on your chest whispers back at you. This means nothing. It is a declarative statement. They just want you to know they're still there, a linguistic manifestation of the dance they do every time you hit a bump in the road.

"Bitch tits," the crowd cheers. By this they mean you're one of them.

FUCK HAPPINESS

Everyone in the stands is a middle-aged man. They're all shirtless. They start a wave of fetid breast meat that fans the field.

The wave blows you into an origami pushcart. Bundy tosses you the football and starts speaking in English translated to Japanese, then Portuguese, then back to English. "Why did you not take my dog?" he asks.

You speak in the phonetic equivalent of ransom note font. "Bitch tits?" you ask him. But that isn't what you mean.

He pulls down his pants. His cock is a pool noodle. It reminds you of Spring, which makes you uncomfortable, so you fall through the pushcart because you're immaterial. You ask Bundy how he ever saw you.

"The manufacture foyer glares intensely through curtains," he says.

You drop into a cauldron or lake or cauldron and lake. Fog rolls through the surrounding trees toward the edge of the water. You hear the drone of chamber flies. They come to feed off the keystrokes you never made on your old Smith Corona. They bathed in the sweat of your fingertips for years, gliding across the starting position, spinning like tops across QWERTY. On some level you know you were supposed to listen to them, but you staved them off with sanity.

The flies lick their appendages. In every direction, thousands of you refracted in black, broken-mirror eyes.

You're paralyzed. You try to scream for help, but your mouth is packed with gauze. You flail wildly, but in your dream it is so slow, so weak. Your will means nothing here.

Your will has never meant anything. This place is just more honest.

The flies encompass you. Al Bundy dressed as a fly or a fly dressed as Al Bundy holds a large maggot over your head. Another fly tips your head back and pushes your jaw until it unhinges involuntarily.

Al Bundy dressed as a fly or the fly dressed as Al Bundy drops the writhing mass into your mouth.

You swallow.

Home rings.

FOUR
FUCK CPS
FUCK YOUR EX-WIFE
FUCK EMPLOYMENT

YOU wake before your alarm goes off to a knock at your door.

Beth.

The clock reads 7:45 a.m. Too early for Beth.

You sit at the edge of your bed. "Hang on."

Your daughter pounds on the bedroom door. "Daddy I gotta go pee!"

"Then do it!"

She holds herself, hopping from foot to foot. "I'm afraid to go alone!"

You open the door. "Where's Tommy?"

She surges past you as you open the door, makes it to the linoleum of the bathroom ... and pisses on the floor. "Tommy wouldn't go with me."

"Get on the toilet! Quick!" you shout.

"Sorry, Daddy!"

It's too late. She's already done. "Where's your bag?"

"I don't know."

"How can you not know? You put it somewhere when you got

here."

Another knock at the apartment door.

"Hang on! Jesus!" you shout, before saying to Karen, "Alright. I'll find your bag."

You storm into the neighboring room and open the main door. Child Protective Services?

The man places his thumb behind his nametag and presses it in your direction. "Dave Edwards. May I come in?"

You roll your eyes. "I have had my kids for one night. One. Night."

The man in the hallway takes off his hat. His bald spot is strangely disarming. "I'm sorry."

You step out of the way. "Come on in."

Karen yells from the other room. "Daddy?"

"Hang on." You start to explain yourself as you rummage through the pile of plastic bags at the far end of your living room. "She had an accident."

"I won't keep you long. We had a call last night. Someone said they smelled pot smoke coming from your apartment."

You finally find Karen's bag under the bags of canned food you bought yesterday. "You want to test me? I'm clean."

He shakes his head. "I know you are."

"Was it Beth?"

He's motionless. "I can't say."

"Christ. She gives me the kids for one night and calls CPS."

"I'm not confirming or denying it was her, but it's not unheard of, a mother in the middle of a custody battle lets the father see the children and tries to use the visit as an opportunity to concoct damning evidence against him. Kid comes home with bruises, smelling like smoke, some complaint like that."

"We're not even having a custody battle." You open the bedroom door. "I'm tossing them in, honey." Karen holds her arms out to catch the underwear, but you know they'll drop into the puddle on the floor. You run them in to her. "Did you wash your hands?" you whisper.

"Who's here?"

"Just a friend. Did you wash your hands?"

"I think so."

You take her hands into yours. They're cold and clammy. "Alright." You hand her the new pair of underwear. "Rinse your feet in the tub before you put the new ones on."

You walk back into the small living room. "We haven't even been split up that long."

The CPS worker is rummaging through your hamper.

"What are you doing?"

He looks up, revealing a pair of your dirty boxers in each hand. "Just checking for residue."

"You aren't going to find what you're looking for in there."

He solemnly drops your boxers back into the hamper. "I believe you're right." He stands up, dusts his jacket off. "I can see you're clean. I just need to fill out the report."

"How many house visits do you make in a day?" you ask.

He pulls a pen out of his coat pocket. "Enough to keep me busy."

"How many do you think are fake, or retaliatory?"

"I have to treat them all as genuine."

"So there's no data?"

"Not that I know of."

You take a roll of paper towels off the shelf in the kitchenette. "I better go clean up the mess."

"I'll see myself out."

In the bathroom, Karen kneels in the puddle, rubbing a full toilet paper roll against the pee.

"Damn it, Karen," you whisper.

"What? I'm cleaning it up!"

You take the toilet paper and throw it into the trash. Urine trickles across the floor. "Rinse your legs off in the tub. Again."

"Again?"

"I told you to rinse your feet off in the tub before changing."

Karen starts to cry.

"It's okay." You want to beat your head against a wall. "Don't cry." *Not while CPS is here. Please don't do this now.*

She nods and sits on the edge of the tub. "Should I get another pair?"

"You're fine." You turn the knob until the water is lukewarm. "Just dip your feet in there real quick. I'll clean up the pee."

As you're soaking everything up, the CPS—agent? person? whatever the fuck you call them—he pokes his head in. "I left a copy on the coffee table. Just wanted to mention quickly. If you want your kids to live with you, they should have their own beds. They'll need their own rooms when they get a bit older, too."

"Thank you. Not really thinking that far ahead, but it is good to know."

He hands you a business card. "Let me know if you need anything."

"Can you set it down?" You nod toward the piss-soaked paper towels on the floor. "Hands are kind of tied." You go back to cleaning the floor, but hear no movement behind you. You turn to check on Mr. CPS.

You swear you catch him leaning in, trying to get a whiff of your ass.

He re-presents the card to you.

"Just set it on my nightstand."

He steps to the edge of the room and drops the card by your bed. "Again. I'm sorry."

"It's fine." You look up at him. "It isn't your fault."

"Most people aren't quite so understanding."

"I get it. Gotta make a living somehow."

He tips his hat and closes the door.

You turn to Karen. "Did he just try to smell my ass?"

"I don't know, Daddy."

Fucking weirdo.

Beth shows up in the afternoon to pick up the kids, all smiles.

You peer through the sliver-sized opening in the front door. "I thought you were coming tomorrow?"

"Let's let them decide."

Great. If they ask to go home, you'll be crushed. If they decide to stay, Beth will hate your face and probably call CPS again. "Kids, your mom is here."

Tommy comes running out of your bedroom, 3DS in hand.

"Aww, Mom!"

Fuck.

"Aww, Mom what?"

"You said we could stay the whole weekend."

Beth straightens her purse. She pulls tight on the strap and glares at you. "Is that what I said?"

"Yes!" He walks back into the bedroom, eyes glazed from excessive screen time.

"I guess they can stay." She tips her head in the direction of the stack of plastic bags. "What you got there?"

"We went shopping last night. Got the kids Lunchables and shit."

"Lunchables *are* shit, Milton." She walks over and starts rummaging through the bags. "You didn't get Karen the ones with pepperoni, did you? You know that makes her puke in her mouth if she sleeps on her back."

"She wanted the nacho ones." Which, incidentally, also make her spew in her sleep.

"What's on the menu for tonight? Hot dogs and Michelob Ultra?"

"Macaroni and cheese."

Beth keeps digging. "You get them vitamins?"

"No, I didn't get them vitamins."

Karen comes running out. "He got us musical toothbrushes!" She presses the toothbrush against Beth's stomach and turns it on. "You can feel it!"

Beth pushes the brush off her shirt. "It's covered with spit, Karen! Gross."

Karen sticks it back into her mouth. "It plays princess songs!" she mumbles.

Beth pats her on the head. "Go play, dear."

Karen runs off.

"Don't run with shit in your mouth, Karen!" Beth turns to you. "They need vitamins."

"Come back with vitamins, then."

"I'm fucking broke." Beth rummages through the bags. "Jiffy?" She holds a jar of peanut butter up. "I haven't seen this in ages."

You shrug. "It's what I always get."

"I asked my brother about it and he laughed at me, said it never existed." She holds it at her waist, spins the container slowly. "You mind if I hang on to this?"

Karen runs into the room, hands you an old *Rugrats* tape you found at a garage sale last summer. "It's broke, Daddy."

It's only missing a few minutes of the last episode. You must have forgotten to patch it back up. "I'll try to fix it in a bit." You wave her back to the TV. "I'm broke too, you know," you say.

"Then get a job. You know, like the one I've been working for the past four years to help put your nutty ass through college."

"I'm trying."

"Where'd you apply?"

"Pharmacy."

"Bullshit. They're not even accepting applications."

"They took mine."

"You're so full of shit." She holds up the jar of Jiffy. "I'm taking this. You can take it off the child support you owe." She waves to Karen. "Bye kids. See you tomorrow."

The door slams shut.

Karen switches her toothbrush off and on, staring at it intently. "Bye, Mom," she says.

The next morning you drop your kids off with Beth. She comes out in ratty sweats and mascara running down her cheeks from the night before. She lights a cigarette and crosses her arms. She won't even look at you.

So you didn't apply at the pharmacy. What's Beth going to do, call fucking CPS on you again? Rub her cunt on your face until you cum? She's got nothing.

You've got nothing.

Dad was right. You should have gone for nursing or something that started paying the bills after only a few years.

You head home to finish up the work on *Country Cuzzins*. You clip out a section near the end of the movie and insert clips from *Rugrats*, *Faces of Death*, and a few selections from *Married with Children* and the evening news. You toss the tape in your rewinder and let it spin for twenty seconds. You pop it out and watch your work.

The images are barely visible, and the auto-tracking can barely keep up with the tape you used to connect the random sequences, but it's all there.

You spend the rest of the afternoon running from store to store:

Dunkin Donuts gives you a tall order of hot bullshit with half a dozen espresso excuses about cutting hours.

Dollar Tree's got a help wanted sign in the window, but they tell you they've run out of applications once you walk inside.

P&C is going out of business.

And Agway . . . man, fuck Agway.

You run through the other small businesses. What else is there? Everything mom and pop has been pushed out of town, replaced by Sunoco and all the other corporate fuckwads.

That leaves two places: Unleavened, the Christian coffee shop, and Super Center. You've avoided Unleavened for years, ever since the owner's wife wrote a scathing article about homosexual marriage for the college paper. But you'll try anything before Super Center. You love shopping there, but no amount of money is worth the abject torture of pressing palms with obese colleagues until sweaty chicken farts escape from beneath the folds of your joined hands while singing odes to employment.

By the time you get to Unleavened your ears are burning. You walk in and see a young girl working behind the counter. She smiles at you . . . and walks away to bus a table, leaving you with the owner, Mike Pisculli.

He does not smile. He hatefully churns out a caramel macchiato while eyeing you. "Can I help you?"

"I was wondering if maybe I could help you."

"You the bean wholesaler?"

"No. Just looking for a job. I used to go to college with your wife."

He glares at the foam rising to the top of the biodegradable paper cup.

Shit. He probably thinks you slept with her. You should have said you used to go to their church. You didn't, but it would have been a better lead in.

"Next month, maybe. Once the college kids thin out I'll lose a few people. Of course, business dies down then too, but if things are still going alright I'll take you."

You decide not to go for the hard sell. A month from now you might still be looking, and it is the most positive response you've had all day. "Okay. Thanks!"

You walk two blocks out of town, past the water tower, to Super Center.

You walk past the Polk High football field. You climb the chain link fence near Super Center, wade waist deep into the cauldron or lake or cauldron and lake from your dreams. You walk through the bottom of the lake to the other side, over divots in the mountain ranges. Micro-valleys.

At the top of a mountain you notice a red tide beating against the back end of Super Center. The collective figure demands from the razorwash backdrop shutterblindness. Static circling, piling upon inordinate checkerboard pillars, uprooting the barren reds in the distance.

A tree at the edge of the parking lot bears application fruit. You take one and walk inside. The security panels scan you for ID. The application auto-populates.

The tile becomes a conveyor belt. Al Bundy dressed as a fly or a fly dressed as Al Bundy takes your application. You tell him what a big fan you are. "I'm a huge fan!" you shout.

Saying nothing, he cradles your application and runs, dropping dead at the 10-yard line. The biggest fly you've ever seen opens a webbed door and vomits on the application. It drinks your application through its proboscis. "Come with me," it buzzes.

"Are you the manager?" you ask.

The fly takes you to a room filled with candy dispensers. It vomits application coins into a token dispenser and gives you 50-cent replicas of your face.

You place a coin into the opening of one machine and turn the dial. As you hear your tiny face crunch under the pressure of the mechanism, a plastic ball rolls out. You open it.

It is empty.

You are empty.

The fly turns your right palm upward and places what looks like a stapler in the center of your hand. You feel a sharp, two-pronged sting. "You're hired," the fly buzzes.

You look down and swear you see something tiny burrow under your skin. "What was that?" you ask.

"Thought leech," the fly responds. "We only activate it when you're on the clock. It's in the union contract."

You rub at the wound, now artificially sealed by some black substance oozing to the surface of your palm. "Okay."

"You're hired," the fly buzzes.

"That's it?" you ask.

"That's it," the fly responds. "You start tomorrow. Stock boy. Night shift."

FIVE
IN THE SUPER CENTER PARKING LOT, YOUR CAR HAS TITS

THE following night, you check your watch as you powerwalk through the front doors. You jog past the seasonal aisles, past the video game section, through the forest of pool noodles, to the stock room. The night shift manager sits with digits crossed, watching twelve security camera monitors. Heavily saturated blue images of your mother cascade across your face.

"Here five minutes and already you're stealing," your boss drones.

You turn your pockets inside out. "I haven't stolen anything."

He points to the screen. "Stealing my time. You can grieve for your dead mother when your shift is over."

"Sorry." Your mom has been dead for years. You didn't even know you were thinking about her. The cameras don't lie, so you think about job stuff. Cardboard boxes and shit. "Where do I punch in?"

Your boss points to a small box on the wall near the exit.

You walk over, place your hand on the screen. The countdown to shift's end begins.

"Grab a dolly and head to Home & Garden." Your boss waves you toward the far corner of the room. "Bob'll give you a hand."

"Bob. He stock the toy aisles?"

"Sometimes."

"I think I met him the other day."

"Great." Your boss waves you out of the room.

You reach for the first dolly in the corner. It's rusted and one wheel wobbles, just like the fucking grocery carts your mom used to have the misfortune of picking. *Don't think about mom. Don't think about mom,* you think to yourself. But by trying not to think about your mom, you think about your mom.

You drag the dolly to home and garden. In aisle three, you run into Bob. "I'm with you tonight."

He slowly lowers his hand to the box cutter in . . . Christ, does this asshole actually have a box cutter holster on his belt? "How's it going?"

"Well, I got a job, so that's a start."

He takes out his box cutter and slices open a large 4x12-foot package on the floor. "Better than nothing."

One by one, the fluorescent lights die until the entire store goes pitch black.

You reach in your pocket for your phone. "I've got a light somewhere here."

Bob grabs your hand and holds it firmly. "We're a dark factory during night shift. No lights," he whispers.

"How are we going to get anything done in the dark?"

"You don't actually *do* anything once the lights go out. You just think about the job." He pulls you out of the aisle. "Come with me." He takes you straight, then left, then straight again.

New car scent and fresh rubber hangs in the air.

You're in the automotive section. "Tires aren't scheduled for maintenance or re-stock tonight. This'll be a good spot to hole up."

You hear him step up onto the shelving.

He turns and whispers. "Reach for my hand. I'll pull you up."

You wave your hand through the darkness until you feel clammy fingertips grasping at nothingness. You place your foot on the lowest row of shelving and Bob pulls you up into the suspended tractor tires. You crawl inside and try to make yourself comfortable.

Several minutes pass. Bob says nothing.

You grow restless. "Are we really just going to sit here all night?"

"Stop talking. You have to think about the job. At least keep it in the back of your head."

"I don't even know what the job entails."

"Sure you do. You've shopped here before. It entails whatever you see day employees doing when you're here."

"So just imagine stocking the shelves and shit?"

"Put some detail into it though. Like don't just think loosely about stocking shelves. Think specifically about which items, where in the store you are."

"Anything else?"

"Wonder when you're going to take a break from time to time to make it more realistic. And when you finally get an actual break, you're free to think about whatever you want to."

And so, for the remainder of the night, you sit in the dark, thinking about working to avoid getting fired for not doing your job.

At 9 a.m. you hear automated mops cut through crude oil residue, the footprints of your mechanical colleagues. The vents kick on and the smell of WD-40 transitions to tea tree oil from aisle six of home and garden.

You stare into the black across from you, wondering if Bob is still there. You never heard him leave, but never heard him breathe or shift. You don't even know for certain if you stayed awake through the entire shift.

The lights come on, blinding you momentarily before you close your eyes. Bob nudges you. "Alright, man. We can talk now. Ready to punch out?"

You lift your lids slowly, start at your feet and work your way up the inside of the tire and out into automotive.

A vibrant sheen reflects the ceiling lights. You've been here thousands of times, and yet you've never seen it so clean.

Bob crawls out of the tire. "Come on. Let's go."

You all but fall out of the tire and rise. "How long have you been here?"

"Long enough." He turns toward home and garden. "Nightly routine hasn't changed much."

"Don't you get bored?"

"Not everybody gets lucky enough to have a job that makes them feel important in life. If you're working some menial shit show, what difference does it make? Keeping busy just passes the time. Being bored makes time crawl, but you innovate. You learn how to make more of it." Bob turns into the aisle where you left your dollies and unpacked boxes the night before. "You ever heard of Siddhartha?"

"No."

"He was the master of doing something by doing nothing. Fucker just sat there for weeks—not eating, not sleeping—until he had an epiphany." Bob moves a display model coffee table on the bottom shelf and stuffs his box behind it. "You know what he realized?"

"What's that?"

"It's all bullshit, man." He drags his dolly behind him, leading the way. "Once you experience ego death, everything is just a big pile of shit." He shakes his head. "Namaste and fuck *me*. Fuck *I*. That's where it's at. The self doesn't matter."

"I'll take your word for it."

Bob turns into the management office. "*I* doesn't exist."

Inside, your boss picks at his proboscis. "He do alright out there?"

"He's handy." Bob pushes his dolly into the corner and punches out.

Your boss turns to you. "He show you the ropes?"

You nod, set your dolly in the corner, and punch out. "I think I got the hang of it."

"Alright. We'll keep you two together then. Enjoy your morning, boys."

You're practically out the door, but you turn to make eye contact. "You too."

Bob follows you through the door. "So what're your plans?"

You're not sure what kind of subtext his question is loaded with, so you scramble for an excuse. "Fucking bed," you say.

"You mind catching me a ride home? I have to pick up a few things near the pharmaceuticals, but I'll make it quick. I'm right in town."

"Sure."

You take Bob to pharmaceuticals. He needs a cart? He needs a cart. Let Bob browse the diuretics and laxatives. You try to look at liquid protein, but Bob already has his cart half filled with five-pound bags of magnesium sulfate and Smooth Moves. How can you do anything but watch in awe?

Bob isn't a discerning laxative customer. When the stock of five-pound bags runs dry, he grabs one-pound bags of citrus and mint aromatherapy Epsom salts not designed for human consumption. You know this because you check the one remaining bag on the shelf. It reads: "not fit for human consumption."

Is he going to soak in it? What the fuck is this guy up to?

Bob heads to the twenty items or less counter. The girl at the counter is thin and pock faced. Her name is Pock Face. Her name is Pock Face because her nametag reads "Pock Face." Her name is "Pock Face" because you objectify the parts of her body that don't carry with them the connotation of sex. Because if her nametag read "Tits O'Sullivan" you'd be overburdened with the guilt of male privilege. She's beautiful and you think you're in love with her. But you've also been lying in a tractor tire for eight hours and your boss is a fly, so you're not sure what love is anymore.

You're standing in line with a man who has forty pounds of laxatives in his cart. You're not sure what anything is anymore.

On some level you wish her nametag read "Tits O'Sullivan."

"You find everything you're looking for?" she asks as she checks out the mint-citrus one-pound bags.

"I had a little trouble finding the crack-cocaine, actually," you joke.

She doesn't smile.

Bob doesn't smile.

You realize you're not smiling either. *Namaste and fuck you too,* you think.

Pock Face rings up the last bag. Bob runs his card through and asks for his employee discount. "Can you ring me up with the 10%?"

"Got your employee ID?"

He digs through his pockets and turns to you. "Can I use yours?"

You reach into your pocket and hand him your employee ID, knowing already the Super Center algorithms will have pegged you as a bulimic by the day's end. You'll be getting coupons for colon cleanse until you die . . .

You think this might not be such a bad thing.

Pock Face swipes the card and hands it back to you. You can't look her in the eyes. You take the card and slide it into your pocket.

"Need any help out?" she asks.

You do. You need help out of the store, through the security panels, out of the parking lot, to the nearest NASA space station, out of your day clothes, into a space suit, and on the nearest shuttle off of this godforsaken planet. You want Pock Face to come with you. You want to populate some alien world with little pock-faced children who write shitty poetry and wonder why the fuck their new friends need to buy forty pounds of Epsom salts. It all starts with one step. That step being you asking for her phone number.

"We're fine," you say. "Thank you."

Bob pushes the cart through the first snow. "Where's your car?"

You can't remember. How did you get here? Do you even have a car? You have a pile of keys on your belt buckle, so it stands to reason you have a car.

You thumb through your keys, of which there seem to be hundreds. "I think it's a Toyota," you say. So you walk through the parking lot until you find a car with the same fucked up "T" symbol as your key.

Key doesn't fit. Car looks too new anyway.

You try car after car. Christ, every other car in the parking lot is a Toyota.

You walk for what seems like miles until you get to the end of the parking lot where one ghost-white, pock-faced fucking Toyota sits. Its name is Pock Face. Its name is Pock Face because the license plate reads "PCK FCE." It wears a green push up bra you're in love with.

The key fits.

You pop the trunk and Bob loads it up with forty pounds of Epsom salts.

You're jealous.

You've never seen her take forty pounds of magnesium sulfate.

You've never seen her. You're quite sure you walked here.

You let Bob in on the passenger side and the two of you ride PCK FCE past the wholesale grocery store, the sock factory, and the cauldron or lake or cauldron and lake from your dream. You remember it being closer to Super Center. You don't remember having a big-titted Toyota named PCK FCE. You decide not to look a gift horse that fucks with your sense of geography in the mouth. Tit-mobile, after all.

You hit the bridge just before the video rental store. "Namaste and drop me off here," Bob says.

You pull over. "You sure?"

"Yeah." Two men run out from under the bridge with ski masks and a rusted shopping cart. "You can always find us at the bridge."

You pop the trunk and watch the men descend on the magnesium sulfate like vultures. They fill the rusted cart and run back down the hill.

Bob reaches in to shake your hand. "See you tomorrow, man."

You shake on it. "I think you will. Yeah."

You pull back onto the pavement and drive less than a block home.

When you get inside, your landline answering machine is aglow with heaps of bullshit. At least that's what Siddhartha would tell you.

First message: "Milton, you ever going to pick up the kids. I've got a date tonight. You fucking—"

Next message: "Hello, Dave here from CPS. Just a quick follow-up to see how things are going. Sorry about the boxer thing today, I—"

Next message: "Milton, this is Mr. Tits Mobile O'Sullivan. You've been driving my wife, PCK FCE, filling her trunk with—"

End of new messages.

You lie down in bed without returning any of the calls. Namaste and fuck everyone.

Fuck your ex-wife.

Fuck Dave from CPS.

There's no way in hell your car's lover left a message on your phone to express concern about its overstuffed trunk.

You make a mental note to check your messages again in the morning.

You almost get out of bed to take the push up bra off the front panel of PCK FCE to see if there's actually a pair of boobs under there.

Instead you adjust the window blanket to mimic the respite evening provides and rub yourself on the bedspread until you fall asleep without having an orgasm.

SIX
DEAD CATTLE DAYCARE

NOT five hours later you wake before the alarm to Beth slamming against your door.

You stumble to the bathroom and toss a palmful of water across your face.

Your ex-wife continues pounding on the door.

Karen tells Beth to stop. "He'll get up," she whispers.

Your morning is Monopoly for deadbeat dads.

You run your hands up and down your face.

You go straight to kid prison.

You do not look in the mirror.

Your wife collects your two-hundred dollars. "Where the fuck were you last night?"

"Working."

She steps into your apartment, tracking mud all over the floor. "I want to see your schedule."

You usher the kids in. "I'll write it down for you tonight."

Beth turns to you. "I want a fucking screen shot. You're not going to use this job to screw me out of a new start."

"What are you talking about? You wanted child support. I'm trying to help!"

"I had a date last night."

"I'm sorry."

Tommy kicks his shoes off and slams the door. "He's a fucking loser, Dad."

Beth pulls the 3DS out of his hands and holds it above her head. "Watch your mouth, mister!"

You head into the kitchenette. "Do I know him?"

She shakes her head and hands the 3DS back to Tom. "You got any coffee?"

"It's Gary," Tom says.

You take a canister of dollar-store coffee out of the cupboard and dump some into a filter you placed in the machine the night before. "Giga Video Gary?"

"He's just working there part time while he's in college."

You flip the switch on the coffee maker. "I already have a degree."

"In Humanities." She drops her purse on the couch and walks into the kitchenette with you. "Where the fuck are the cups?"

"Same place they've always been."

She slams the first cupboard door. "Littering the fucking night stand then?"

You open the cupboard closest to the fridge and hand her a chipped "world's greatest dad" mug. "Why are you so pissed? I'd hate to keep pressing this, but you left me."

"Yes, I did." She tears the coffee pot from the machine and pours herself a cup. "And not fucking once have you asked me to come back."

The machine just keeps pumping coffee all over the heating plate. It sizzles, dries immediately, then begins to smoke.

You place your mug directly under the stream of coffee coming out of the broken machine. "If I thought it was what you wanted, I'd take you back."

She sets her cup down. "Ask me then."

You look down at the counter. "Will you come back?"

"Where's the creamer?" she asks.

"I just have the powdered shit." You hand her the Coffee Mate. You watch her pour a spoonful in her cup and stir the clumps into the vortex-black coffee. "So?"

"So what?" she asks.

"Will you come back?"

She sips at her coffee. "I'll take my chances with Gary." She takes her cup into the bedroom.

"His degree is in Humanities too!" You grab your half-cup from the machine and flip the switch. "Be right back, kids." You follow Beth into the bedroom and close the door. "Are you going to fuck him?"

"I might."

"I don't have to work until tonight." You set your cup down on the nightstand, next to two other cups you haven't picked up since earlier in the week. "We could get your stuff and move you back in right now."

Beth parts the curtains slowly. The second sun of Nibiru refracts through the eyes of an eight-ton rotting cattle corpse in the distance and catches her cheekbones. She's a poor man's Scarlett Johansson, which you mean as a compliment because Scarlett Johansson is a poor man's Scarlett Johansson too, depending on her role.

"Did you do something different with your hair?"

She stares longingly out the window in the direction of Giga Video. "I'm not fucking you."

You stand behind her and take her blond shoulder-length hair into your hands. You let it sift between your fingers. "I mean, wasn't your hair short last time we talked?"

"It's always been like this, stupid."

"It looks really nice."

"When do you want me to pick up the kids?"

"I could really use a bit more sleep."

"I'm not fucking you."

You really want to fuck her. "Yes. We've established that."

"How about I come back tomorrow around six p.m.? That'll give you time to get cleaned up for work. If you need a nap, just tell the kids. They can look after themselves."

"I have to work tonight."

"Well tonight is *your* night. Figure something out."

"When did we agree on this arrangement?"

"Fuck off, that's when."

You take a deep breath, try to change the subject. "You want to come to Super Center with us?"

"No thanks." She sets her cup on the nightstand next to the others. "I'm going to go fuck Gary."

"Jesus, Beth."

"What? I'm just being honest."

"It hurts."

She shrugs. "He wants that fucking porn he let you borrow back too."

You head for the TV, dig through the stack of tapes on the floor. "He recommended it." You stuff it into the hard shell case and hand it to her.

"Sure he did, perv." She heads for the door. "Bye, kids."

They both wave without looking. "Bye, Mom."

Beth closes the door behind her.

"What's a porn?" Tommy asks.

"What's a perv?" Karen asks.

You can tell by the smiles on their faces that they already know, so you ignore them. "Did your mom dye her hair or something?"

Tommy looks confused.

Karen shakes her head. "She's always had Barbie hair, Daddy."

You want to go to the bedroom window and wait for Beth to pull into Giga Video. But you know that'll kill the rage boner in your pants completely, possibly for days or weeks.

You want to know, but you don't want to know.

Your wife fucking Gary is a car crash you can't look away from.

Your wife fucking Gary is a clichéd simile you can't stop using.

Your wife fucking Gary is like the second sun of Nibiru dancing on the glint of a bloated eight-ton cattle corpse.

That afternoon, you take the kids to Super Center.

Tommy and Karen run through the security panels and head for the seasonal aisle. It's almost Christmas, so seven-foot Santas adorn the end shelves. Word balloons dangle above their heads, imploring your children to be good for goodness' sake. Paper Rudolphs with red cotton ball noses wield disarming smiles that distract customers from their black, lifeless eyes. The customers stare away from Rudolph's black, lifeless eyes with black, lifeless eyes. You stare at them with black, lifeless eyes, wondering what they are staring at.

You drag the kids to the toy aisles. Bobsleds replace pool noodles. Your children beat your ankles with bobsleds until your blood-soaked wool socks unravel from your legs. Winter is here. It reminds you of the last time you were ever truly happy. Her name was Beth. She had short black hair or shoulder-length blond hair. She looked like Juliette Lewis in *What's Eating Gilbert Grape?* or Scarlett Johansson in *Ghost World*. She ate Jif or Jiffy peanut butter.

She did not beat you with bobsleds. She made you love life enough to stop writing. She was your poetry.

Your children continue to beat your ankles. Tommy takes the jagged bobsled runner and cuts across your shinbones. The blood spurts onto the fire started by your leg hair during your last visit. You want to laugh. You tell them to never stop.

Your boss rounds the corner and hovers above you.

He smells it, you think. By "it" you mean your disappointment.

He smiles.

You smile.

He vomits on the puddle of blood accumulating at your feet. Your children hop on their bobsleds and fly down the aisles as your boss drops to his knees and feeds on you. "You're early," he slurps.

"I'm not sure I'll make it in tonight. I have the kids."

Your boss stands, snaps his fingers, and waves your kids into the back office.

You stumble after them as they glide gently to the back office on puddles of you.

"We all have lives, Milton," your boss says as he takes a seat on the edge of his desk. "I have kids. You have . . . these things." Your boss opens his top drawer and takes a swaddled mass out of the desk. "I'm just saying, we've got daycare, night care. Whatever. We can make something work." He holds the writhing mass of blankets out. "Meet my youngest."

You were wrong. There are no blankets. The larva is just a muscled mass of gyrating flesh.

Karen pokes its center. "It's cute," she says.

"Would you like to play with him?" your boss asks.

Karen looks back at you. You shake your head as subtly as possible. "I might drop him," she says.

"Understandable." Your boss stuffs the maggot back into his top drawer. He folds his appendages and looks at you. "So what's this you said about not making it in tonight?"

"Well, if we have daycare I might be able to swing it."

"It's out front."

"The fireworks tent?"

"Right next to it."

"Okay." You point at the bobsleds, then out to the aisles. By this you mean, "Put those fucking bloody bobsleds back."

Tommy flips you the bird. By this he means, "I'll get right on that." He takes Karen by the hand and they drag their bobsleds back out to the toy aisles.

"When you want me here?" you ask.

Your boss rounds his desk and plops down in his chair. "You've got a few hours." He throws you a few tokens. "Why not take the kids out to those cheap toy dispensers then show them around daycare?"

You follow the trail of blood back to Tommy and Karen. "You guys want to get something from those machines in the front?"

Karen claps. "Can I pick myself?"

You toss her a token. "Sure."

Tommy holds out his hand. "Fine."

The junk toy dispensers stretch miles above the children's range of sight. They walk up to the digital prompt and scan through the alphabetized list of themed dispensers. Karen scrolls through the list and stops on youmojis. The dispensers rearrange themselves like the tiles on a sliding puzzle until the youmoji vending machine is at eye level with Karen. She slides her token in.

Tommy tugs at her shoulder. "You used my token!" Karen turns the dial. "It doesn't matter."

Tommy holds his token out. "This one's Karen's."

"Just use her token and trade toys."

"I don't want a youmoji!" He pouts. "They're for girls."

The plastic capsule pops out of the youmoji vendor. Karen opens it, discarding the plastic shell on the ground. She holds up a Tommy youmoji. "I got Tommy's face?"

"I tried to tell you!" Tommy shouts.

Karen screams. "I hate your face!" She lets Tommy's face fall onto the floor, then steps on it.

You look up and Tommy's face is flattened. "I think she broke my nose," he says.

You scrape Tommy's youmoji off the tiled floor. "Karen. You are so fucking grounded!"

Karen bursts into tears.

You make a note to yourself: never ground your children in public.

You drag them by the hands to the daycare center near automotive.

Flies circle the top of the structure, descending to pull their larvae from the cranial cavity. You enter with your kids through the opening in the mouth. A chamber fly checks your employee ID at the back of the throat, and you descend into distended innards. The walls writhe with life squirming just below the surface.

Karen runs her free hand across the slick wall. "I bet we'll make a lot of new friends here, Tommy."

"So what. Mom and dad won't let them stay with us anyway."

"We might, but they'd have to bring their own carcass." You try to backpedal, but there's no way to fully revoke your offer. "And a tarp."

"See, Tommy. I told you he's cooler than Mom!"

As the three of you walk into the emptied intestinal hallways, you beam with pride.

In the large intestines you find a small room for the humans. The entrails are sealed with a polyurethane-like coating to prevent accelerated decomposition. A fan pumps fresh air into the room from outside.

"How long do you think this giant cow has been here?" Tommy asks.

You shrug. "I never noticed until yesterday." You ruffle the hair on Tommy's head. "You'll watch your sister while I'm working?"

He sighs. "Yeah.

"Alright, kids. I'm heading back in then."

On the way back out of the cattle mouth, you hand the chamber fly your number. "Call me if there are any problems."

He takes the small sheet and tucks it into his pocket.

You follow the red puddles of you back to the bobsleds and take a deep breath before stepping in with your boss.

SEVEN
GHOST JOB

"**Y**OU'RE back." Your boss lurches over his desk, running his rear legs over the underside of his wings. "Close the door."

Bob is seated, facing the boss.

You close the door slowly, shutting out the fluorescent light of the storefront. All that is left is the ghost-like glow of the exit sign and the flickering monitor on your boss' desk. "What's up?"

Your boss continues grooming himself. "One of your fuckers was thinking off the job last night." He pounds the desk with his front leg.

Bob turns to you with his teeth gritted and eyebrows raised. "It is hard to keep the mind on task, sir."

Your boss scratches his ... chin? What the fuck is he scratching? You can't tell if he is grooming or contemplating something. He flips his monitor with his second, left leg. There it is, a grainy video of Bob sucking your dick in the middle of home and garden. At first you think he's deep throating, but when he pulls away you realize your dick is just amazingly tiny in this fantasy.

"That is not my penis!" you shout, realizing suddenly your manhood is not in question.

"Is that a declaration of innocence?" Your boss crosses his

front legs. "Because I'd assume it wasn't your dick in either case. If it was his fantasy, he'd make it smaller than his, and if it was your fantasy, you'd make it bigger than it actually is."

"What exactly are you getting at here, sir?" Bob asks.

"That one of you has a tiny dick. And we're about to find out who."

You unzip your pants.

You *really* need this job.

Bob shakes his head. "There's no way I'm exposing myself to the two of you."

"Alright, tiny." Your boss crawls off the front of his desk onto the floor. "I think we can safely assume you're the culprit."

"It wasn't me!" Bob squirms in his chair as your boss crawls up his legs.

Your boss uses his proboscis like another leg as he comes face-to-face with Bob. "Then pull it out. Milton's already flashed his meat."

Bob turns quickly to look.

Too quickly.

"It *was* you!" your boss buzzes.

"No! No!" Bob rocks in his chair against the weight of your boss, in vain.

Your boss drops his proboscis on Bob's abdomen and vomits a thick stream of digestive fluids onto Bob's lap.

Bob braces the arms of the chair and shudders violently. "Namaaasttttaaaahhhhh!"

Your boss tips the chair backwards and crawls up onto Bob.

Bob keeps screaming: "Namaste and fuck me! Namaste and fuck you and the horse you rode in on! Namaste and holy fuck, are you actually going to eat me while I'm trying not to fucking die you fucking fly fuck?!"

You avert your eyes as your boss levels his proboscis over Bob's face and heaves again.

The screaming stops.

When you look back, what's left of Bob twitches in a bilious pool of stomach juices.

"I'll clean this up." Your boss shakes his head. "Not a word,

Milton. Got it?"

You step back slowly. "Sure." You look at the pile of Bob. "Where do you want me tonight?"

He waves you out the door. "Same as last shift."

The store goes black as you walk through the office door. You peer out of the aisle and try to memorize the route to automotive. It looks like a straight shot six aisles and then a left, so as soon as it is dark, you dart to the respite only tractor tires can provide.

You vomit as quietly as possible.

Bob is dead.

You climb inside and try not to think about Bob. You don't think about alive Bob. You don't think about dead Bob. You try not to think about suck-your-dick Bob, but this becomes increasingly hard as something keeps tugging at your jeans. You swat the sensation away, but it keeps returning. Finally you whisper, "Fuck off."

It tugs at your shirt. You swat at it, but there's nothing there. You ruffle your shirt and the sensation begins tracing letters on your stomach. The first stroke is a straight line.

Please be PCK FCE, you think, but the straight line curves into a B, and you already know, somehow, it's Bob. "Alright. Alright," you whisper. "I fucking know who it is."

Ghost Bob begins tracing letters on your stomach. "N . . . A . . . M"

You pull down your shirt. "Yeah. Yeah. Fucking namaste. Why don't you fuck off to nirvana?"

"I have unfinished business," you hear. "Now think about your job. I need to talk to you once we're on break."

You focus on your shoes scuffling across the tiling. You think about the sound of cardboard and masking tape being peeled apart. You think about drill bits and other machines rolling past you as you try to work.

You think about your break until you're finally on break.

"Were you really thinking about sucking me off?" you ask Ghost Bob.

"You're not going to call human resources, are you?"

"You're dead."

"I'm still employed though."

"No, I'm not going to call human resources."

"I was going to ask you if I could on the way home, but I could tell you like PCK FCE," Ghost Bob replied.

You both fall silent as something rolls by on thick tread.

"Mop bot," Ghost Bob says. "They come through a few times a night."

You think about your ex. You estimate it is about time for Giga Video Gary to get off work. You wonder if your ex is fucking Gary.

"You ever had a ghost job before?" Ghost Bob asks.

"I never even thought ghosts were real."

"You want to try it? It's not really gay if the ghost you're with has no body."

It has been a long time—too long—since you've felt the touch of another. "That sounds fair." You unzip your pants and Ghost Bob encompasses your pleasure rod with ghost vapor and ghosts it right down to the base.

You've never been ghosted like this before.

You've never been ghosted before at all.

Is that a thing, being ghosted?

You try to pump, but there's no resistance. You try to apply head pressure, but there's nothing to hold onto. You just have to sit there and let Ghost Bob ghost your cock until your break is over.

When the break is over, you still haven't come. So while your dick gets ghosted you think about pocket lint and shipping forms and surplus goods that don't fit on the display shelves. You feel the buildup to climax while you think about your nametag and steel utility knife holsters. It inches down your lifeline, through your back, crawling toward your balls.

A thick lather begins to build on the surface of your skin.

A sudsy discharge builds on every inch of your body as you climax, presumably from your pores.

"What the fuck?" You feel the foam under your shirt. "What is this shit?" You feel the small bubbles popping between the crevices of your body. "What a fucking mess."

"Relax, man." Ghost Bob laughs. "It's normal."

You scrape the foam off your neck and jerk your wrist, casting the discharge to the floor. "Wish you would have warned me I was going to sweat like a fucking horse." You wipe more away from your face and smear it on one of the tires. "Fucking gross."

"It's not gross. Smell test, brah."

You pull your hand to your nose reluctantly. "Flowers?"

"Roses, dude." Ghost Bob ghosts you on the shoulder. "That's not just sweat. It's essence of the soul."

You fluff the substance between your thumb and forefinger. It pops and crackles like crisped rice. It feels light and airy like bubble bath. You inhale again. "It smells really good, actually."

"That's Siddhartha's reward. You just made a bit of the universe pure again."

You don't fully understand what Ghost Bob means by Siddhartha's reward, but you just climaxed flowery universe purity through your sweat glands, which basically calls everything you've ever known into question.

And you've learned as of late not to ask questions. Not about the important stuff, anyway.

"You better get back to thinking about your job," Ghost Bob echoes. "But I want to introduce you to a few of my friends once your shift is over."

You wonder if their universe purity smells like flowers too. You wonder if they'll ghost your dick in a paranormal three-way. Between thoughts of wood glue and display cases, you manage an "Okay."

The lights kick on after an hour of watching images dance behind your eyelids. For as long as you can remember, those images have always been predominantly formless. Like clouds, they emulate actual shapes, but your imagination has to close the gap between the formless colors roiling across a black backdrop and the meaning you want to pull from those formless colors.

But tonight the Rorschach test fails you. There is no room for imagination. Tonight the purple-red colors flow slowly like crude oil across velvet black. You don't just see the colors. You smell them. They smell like semen and formaldehyde.

Purple-red smells like birth and death, but it *is* wood glue, or maybe what wood glue feels like if emotions were colors. Your mind keeps tugging you in the direction of your mother, but purple-red is not your mother. This becomes your mantra. "Purple-red is not your mom. Purple-red is not your mom." You repeat as the lights slowly bake your eyelids.

You open your eyes. It is time to leave.

But you can't leave. Beth never brought the fucking peanut butter back, and you suspect she might come back for another jar. On some primal level you fear that may be the only thing she's feeding the kids. So after you drop the dolly off, you head to the aisle that smells like coffee and look for the Jiffy.

But there's no Jiffy.

You pore over the shelves. Then you run your thumb over each jar that marks a transition from one brand to another.

No Jiffy.

You see a woman pricing bread behind you. You tap her on the shoulder. "I can't find the Jiffy."

She turns. "Jiffy Lube's on Main Street, hon."

"No." You point behind you. "The peanut butter."

"You mean Jif," she says matter-of-factly.

But you don't mean Jif. So you kneel down beside her and look her in the eye. "No. I mean Jiffy. I just bought a jar here a week ago."

"I've been stocking these shelves since this store came into town. No Jiffy. Sorry."

You toss two shatterproof jars of Jif into your basket and head to self-checkout.

You roll the first jar across the scanner. The machine beeps and displays your purchase total. You slide the next jar across the glass. "Fuck Jif," you mumble in the same tone as the scanner. And you mean it.

Fuck Jif. Fuck Jiffy. And fuck your wife.

You pack your items in a plastic bag—fuck the bag and plastic in general, too—and head for PCK FCE. You throw the peanut butter into your trunk. Something shifts behind you. A chill runs down your spine. Almost instinctually you raise your hands and close your eyes.

Nothing.

You turn slowly.

It's Dave from CPS with his nose about an inch from your asshole. He notices you and pretends to shine his shoe. "Just got a little dirt on there." He smiles.

"Why do you keep trying to smell my ass!?" you scream.

Your neighbor, Mrs. Hendrick, passes by as your voice echoes through the parking lot. She stops and stares until she places you in her mental repository of perverts, then realizes you're also housed in her repository of kindly neighbors as well.

She turns up her nose and rushes away with her shopping cart.

That's the last time she'll ask you to carry in her groceries.

Fuck Mrs. Hendrick anyway, the old judgmental bag.

Dave backs away on bended knee. "I'm sorry. I was just . . . it's part of the investigation."

"Really?"

He nods.

"Part of your job description is following people around and trying to smell their ass?"

"Don't question my methods." He stands and adjusts his jacket. "Good day, sir."

You close your trunk, wait for Dave to get out of range, and head back to the bloated cattle near the fireworks. You walk inside. "Kids alright?" you ask without looking at the doorfly.

The doorfly nods, flips another page in its magazine.

You walk down the esophagus into the stomach. Your children are in the third compartment. "Hey, guys."

Tommy tosses a handful of Legos onto the floor and runs over to you. "Can we leave?"

"Yeah. I'm done."

Karen stands in front of the dolly dream house.

"Come on, honey." You inch toward her, noting the faint throbbing at the corner of her head. "Karen?"

"I made a new friend," she says. "It kind of hurts."

You spin her around. A fist-sized maggot writhes at the side of her head. You tug at it.

"Can it come home with us?" she asks.

You pull at it again. "Guess it's going to have to."

"It's going to eat your brain." Tommy slaps the larva. It plants itself firmly on Karen's head and continues writhing.

"It is a she," Karen says. "And she's got a name."

You crouch down and look at it closely. "What is its name, honey?"

"Beth." Karen strokes the maggot and smiles. "Like Mommy."

You stand. "Well, that seems fitting." *Since she is a fucking parasite just like your little friend there.*

"So can she stay the night?"

You head for the neighboring stomach compartment. "We'll see."

You stop short of the front teeth at the entrance. "She's, she's coming with us."

The doorfly nods and turns another page in his magazine.

As you herd the little ones into PCK FCE, you wonder whose kid is attached to your kid. Karen leans against the glass and the maggot sounds like the window cleaner at your father's old office.

You want the maggot gone. You want it dead.

You turn the rear view away from Karen and focus on the road. But every time you close your eyes, the purple-red squirms like dying larvae. What unnerves you the most is that the image brings you comfort. Until you get home.

When you pull in the driveway, you dig the peanut butter out of the trunk and make the kids go up in front of you. This is standard protocol. When you leave the kids come down the stairs after you in case they fall. When you come home the kids go up before you in case they fall. So you know the maggot didn't fall off in the driveway or on the stairs, but you look twice anyway, because when Karen gets inside, the fucking larva is gone.

You're relieved and terrified at the same time. What if that fucking thing was your boss'?

You head back down the stairs. The front porch is eerily quiet.

The flies—the little flies that adorn the windows like living blinds—are gone.

You step closer to the windows.

No carcasses. No shit stains dotting the glass.

The flies aren't gone. They never were.

Perhaps Karen's friend met the same fate.

After you comb the stairs leading to your apartment, the driveway, and under your car (even though you saw the fucker on Karen's head all the way up the stairs), you call Karen and Tommy down to do one more sweep. You wait at the bottom of the stairs as they get their shoes back on. "It isn't in one of your shoes, is it?" you scream up.

"No!" they both shout.

"Coats?"

The kids shimmy into their winter jackets. "Nope."

"Alright, come on down then. Let's take one more look."

Tommy steps through the doorway and jogs down. Karen slams the door behind her, turns . . . and there's the larva on the side of her head.

What the fuck?

"Karen, are you fucking with me?" you ask.

She shakes her head.

The larva hunkers down.

You point to it.

Karen reaches up. "There she is."

"Alright. Well, mystery solved."

Karen opens the door and kicks her shoes off. You follow Tommy and lock the door behind you.

. . . and the larva is gone again.

"Goddamnit, Karen!" You grab her firmly by the head and look where the larva should be. "Where is it now?"

"I didn't do anything with it, I swear!" she cries.

You let her go. "It's okay. I'm sure she'll come back. Maybe she just likes to play hide and seek."

Karen smiles. "I bet that's it."

Tommy unravels your bag from Super Center in the kitchenette. "Aw, man," he moans.

"What's *your* problem?"

"Jiffy sucks, dad."

You step closer to get a good look at the packaging.

Fucking Jiffy.

"You find that in the cabinet?"

He pulls out the other jar. "Got it out of your bag."

You store this in your "what the fuck" repository, item two, just below "where the fuck is Karen's larva?

EIGHT
THE CULT OF
FOUR TEMPERAMENTS

YOU lie in bed that evening, thinking about your kids who believe themselves too old or distant to sneak into your bed at night to snuggle up. You leave your door ajar, knowing they'll likely slip through to hit the bathroom in the wee hours of the morning. They will knock quietly on the inside of the door, peer in, and then head for the toilet. They'll plop down there for a short while, bemused by social mandates nobody explained to them but that they've somehow come to understand or construct on their own. They'll regret the absence of bedtime stories, but they'll outgrow that longing permanently. Each time they come in, you will watch them out of the corner of your eye, hoping they'll slip under the covers beside you and ask you to read them Dr. Seuss. But you will never ask them because rejection has become that much of a deterrent in your life. Your fear of being told no has become so strong, you can barely acknowledge wanting, let alone making your wants heard.

So the closest you all get to one another is pissing and shitting in the dark, scuttling through the half-lit hallways to and from one another, slowly falling out of one another's orbit as if age was a literal marker of distance.

Each year their knocks get quieter. Their trips to the bathroom get fewer and further between. Eventually they avoid you like the plague. You know this because Karen used to jostle you until you woke before peeing. Now she knocks cautiously and darts into the bathroom without saying a word.

Tommy stopped knocking altogether last year. The first time he stayed with you after Beth left, you caught him pissing in the kitchenette sink. You assume that, given his current trajectory, by the time he is twenty-five he'll be a rare comet passing by at a distance every decade or so. You'll stay out all night with a six-pack of beer waiting for him to cross your path on a cloudless night, and he'll just drop by to piss in your sink.

Around 1:30 a.m. Karen tugs at your cave-blanket.

You roll over, half awake. "Toilet paper's under the sink."

Another tug.

You open your eyes.

It isn't Karen.

It's Ghost Bob. "They took our tires."

"Christ, man. My kids are here!" you whisper. "If they see you, you'll scare the shit out of them!"

Ghost Bob sits down beside you on the bed. "I didn't know you had kids."

"We only worked together for one night."

"Feels like a lifetime."

"Yeah. Fighting to stay awake in the darkness seems to have that effect." You sit up and lean against the wall. "What do you want?"

He pulls back the blankets. "Just a quick Ghost Bob on your meat knob."

You throw the blankets at him and roll to your feet. "Kids. Here. Not happening."

Ghost Bob reaches down and picks up your jeans. "I'm just kidding." He lobs your pants to you. "Get dressed. I want you to meet the guys."

You begin the brief one-leg-at-a-time dance into your acid-wash pants. "Now?!"

"Hard to catch them during the day."

"My kids are here."

"So I've heard."

"I can't leave them." You revise. "Very long."

Ghost Bob hovers into your bathroom. "Tell you what, I'll phase in and out to check on them. Every five minutes." He ghosts a bottle of Robitussin out of your medicine cabinet and ghosts it into his pocket. "If anything seems off, you can run home. We're just going to the bridge." He starts rummaging through your sink cabinet. "You got any Epsom salts?"

"There's no way you used all those bags."

"I ran out last night."

"You were dead last night. What the hell do you do with that shit?"

"Expel impurities."

"That much Epsom salts, I'm surprised there's anything left of you, let alone impurities."

"The body has a threshold for both purity and impurity, but the soul . . ." He raises his finger. "The soul is a porous interface between the mind, body, and the impurities of the universe. As such, there is always impurity to expel."

"Cool story, bro." You try to drag Ghost Bob to his feet. "Don't have any shit salt. Sorry. Let's go."

You have lived in this town since you were two years old. In all the years you have been here, this bridge—the bridge you now stand on—has never changed. It has maintained the same puke-green color straight from a Brady Bunch shag carpet, with only a smattering of rust. Rain has never managed to wash away the small spot of blood where you hit a fawn right after getting your license. The names etched into the concrete underbelly were still just as prevalent as the spray paint tags from the three-day "gang" dispute over which cluster of warring juggalos would call themselves the Insane Clown Posse. As you duck under the overpass, you're ashamed dead relics of pop culture still remain here while the world around you has passed them by. This shitty little bridge in this shitty little town, this was white trash Neverland. Nothing here changed, except Pan himself, who was now a homosexual ghost named Bob with a penchant for astral projection hand jobs. Well, nothing here changed except Pan and the weird old guy feeding a burning barrel with Schauss pink sea foam stigmata.

Ghost Bob floats to the edge of the fire. "Dave, I want to introduce you to someone." Ghost Bob waves you over.

"I'd shake your hand, but . . ." He holds up his arms. The foam on his hands crackles over the flames, dissipating into the evening sky. Dave turns to face you.

You blink twice. "This is who you want me to meet? The ass sniffer from CPS?"

"You tried to sniff his ass?" Ghost Bob hovers between you and Dave. "I thought we were going to rely on more subtle methods of recruitment?"

"It was a decision made in haste."

You point accusingly. "So you admit it?"

"Of course." Dave runs his hands over the burning barrel. The faint smell of roses fills the air as foam oozes from his open wounds. He eyes Ghost Bob. "I knew you were somehow related to our work. Your door is a bridge between the current state of chaos in the world and the state of order we're trying to produce. How else was I going to know if you were our melancholic?"

"Give him time to explain," Ghost Bob whispers in your ear. "This dude knows what's up."

You scan the perimeter, looking for copious amounts of Epsom salts. "What do you guys have going on down here, anyway?"

"We're trying to make the world a better place. Or rather, we're trying to get the world to revert back to its natural state." Dave squeezes the tiny bubbles emanating from his wounds. They pop and squeal like a chorus of baby hummingbird micro farts. "The world has been overburdened by entropy for too long. The effects are imperceptible to most, but there are pockets of clarity, places immune to entropy. I have to believe the earth is trying to defend itself against entropy's invasive ether, because the people born in those pockets are negatively polarized. Whereas most people feed off order, the negatively polarized feed off entropy." He releases his grip on the foam and it drops into the flames. They dance frantically, adorned in Schauss pink. "This foam is the byproduct of a negatively polarized soul, a soul running off entropy. The foam is materialized order."

"How do you get it to come out of your hands like that? Can you control it?" *Please say yes,* you think, fearing you may have inadvertently signed on for a lifetime of being covered in Schauss pink stains.

"It depends on your temperament. If you are Bob's replacement, then you may get to a point where you can control it. But you're melancholic, so your body processes entropy via natural bodily functions. I'm sanguineous, so I must bleed myself of order."

Ghost Bob floats unsteadily to your side. "Of the four temperaments, yours is the most unfortunate. The choleric vomit materialized order. The phlegmatic cough it up. Dave bleeds himself. They all have to induce the process. But the melancholic expels impurity through . . . various avenues."

"What do you mean 'various' avenues?"

"Well, sweat, tears . . . maybe excrement sometimes . . . could come out of your ears." Ghost Bob turns to Dave. "It comes out of their ears sometimes, right?"

Dave nods. He takes his hand out of the fire and places it onto your shoulder. It does not burn. "But you're also very important. You signal to the rest of us when we should induce our process. Your body suggests the frequency with which the planet must be purged of entropy, so we need to know when you begin to foam up."

You take a moment to process everything you're being told.

1. The planet is oversaturated with entropy. Check.

2. There are some pockets of resistance on the planet. Check.

3. People born in those pockets seem to filter entropy out of the ether and produce order, kind of like trees filter carbon dioxide and produce oxygen or some shit. Also check.

4. You are one of these people, and you're going to exude foam from every orifice for the rest of your life, because there's LOTS of fucking entropy out there and apparently your body has been single-handedly tasked with cleaning it up.

That last one—the one about sweating, crying, and shitting ad infinitum—that one kind of gets you.

You think back to your second-year lessons on monomyth. Like any archetypal hero about to delve into a hero's journey, you want out. This is your first trial on the road of many, but this isn't some Peter Parker bullshit where you're afraid of the responsibility that comes with power. You're not Luke Skywalker, dreaming of adventure until you're all but forced into a world greater than your own.

You are a working-class deadbeat dad, born within a pocket of entropy-resistant space, destined to ooze materialized order to preserve the cosmic balance of your home planet. Your herald was a homosexual ghost who called you to action with an astral blowjob in the automotive section of Super Center until you were covered with purity foam.

Your wise man appears to be a CPS worker with a messiah complex and a penchant for sniffing buttholes.

. . . and a vulture just walked up to you, downed a bottle of Robitussin, and started hacking up foam on your shoe.

You have no idea who or what the fuck he's supposed to be.

You kick the vulture off your shoe.

"That's Ed." Dave reaches into his pocket, pulls out a bottle of Robitussin DM, and tosses it to the vulture. "He's our phlegmatic."

"Who's the choleric?"

"His shift will be ending shortly."

"Like you're finding someone to replace him?"

Ghost Bob points over his shoulder. "No, he works at the Giga Video. He'll be down in a bit."

"No." You shake your head. "No fucking way. Not Giga Video Gary."

"You know him?"

"He's fucking my wife!"

In the distance, you hear a voice. "Your ex-wife."

It's fucking Giga Video Gary. He walks down to the fire barrel and warms his hands. "And I didn't fuck her. She just told you that to piss you off."

"Are you dating her?"

Gary pulls a small vial of ipecac syrup out of his pocket. "Order is my mistress." He unscrews the cap and downs the ipecac.

A sense of relief washes over you. Then something stirs inside you. You hate your ex-wife for trying to make you jealous. You always thought Gary was an alright guy. He always asked about your kids, your research . . . your wife. But the nonchalant way he addressed you tonight, it seems uncharacteristic of the Giga Video Gary you knew before.

The bitch ruined him for you. You'll never see him the same way again, and you still don't know if you trust him when he tells you not to worry. Order might be his mistress, but order can't suck your dick or stomp on your spine with a pair of Hoka One Ones like Beth can.

"I gotta go," you say.

"Don't leave yet," Ghost Bob pleads.

"No, I have to go to the bathroom."

Dave nods in the direction of the bridge. "There's a little spot under the bridge out of view. Just make sure you go directly onto the ground. Don't go on the concrete."

You run for the small enclave under the bridge and pull down your pants. You feel instant relief, but you hear nothing.

It's like you're pissing air.

You look down. A large pile of foam gathers below you . . . on the concrete.

"Are you okay?" Dave asks.

"I . . . went on the concrete."

"Scrape it onto the ground when you're done. Mother Earth needs nourishment."

"I'm not touching it!"

Dave cups his mouth with his foam-soaked hands and shouts. "There's not a drop of urine in that. It smells like roses. It is bacteria free. It's cleaner than water."

"You spoon it onto the ground then."

"I'm trying to feed the sky. We have to work together. The more we do this, the less you'll go in the future."

Your stomach knots. "Oh God."

Your intestines constrict. Sharp pains shoot from your abdomen to the back of your head, like the ass cramps you used to get in high school. Your legs almost buckle as you brace yourself against the bridge's concrete foundation. "This . . . this doesn't feel right."

Ghost Bob massages your shoulders. Don't fight it.

The pain localizes in your colon. Your chocolate starfish quivers.

You pull down your pants.

You soul shit.

"Wondrous," Dave remarks, smiling.

"This really doesn't feel right!" You try to circle around the pile of foam as you continue to soul shit the world back to a state of equilibrium. You kick at the foam while bracing yourself against the steel beam behind you to no avail. "This isn't working!" You squat-walk out into the open, leaving a trail of foam in your wake. Gary vomits into the burning barrel, Dave wafts his hands over the flames, and the fucking vulture coughs up a lung into the river below. *What a bunch of fucking idiots.*

Twenty minutes later you want to leave, but you can't stop shitting. "Does it ever end?"

Dave nods. "When the four elements are satiated."

You look down to see if you're done, because you hear and feel nothing. You are not done, but the trail of foam behind you is gone. The earth has not only accepted your offering, it devours the foam hungrily and beckons you for more. Ghost Bob hovers in behind you. "You may want to just lay down. I'll wake you when it's over."

"Are you fucking serious? How long does this shit last?"

"A couple of hours . . . sometimes days."

"Fucking *days*?"

"If you can't get time off, Depends work really well."

"You have to be kidding me!"

Ghost Bob astral pats your shoulder. "Just try to rest."

You slowly crouch onto the ground and cradle your legs in a fetal position. "Will you let me know when I stop shitting?"

Ghost Bob nods. "Of course."

A tear streams down your cheek onto the ground. Then you feel it: an explosive burst of rose-scented fluff billows out of your anus.

Ghost Bob astral strokes your head. "Don't get too upset.

You're melancholic. Your sadness feeds the cycle."

"But I'm always fucking sad," you cry.

"Then look at it this way: the more disillusioned you are, the faster it will all be over."

"You think?"

Ghost Bob grins. "I know."

You close your eyes and think about your ex-wife. You think about Gary. Your kids. Your shitty job. Again, you feel the surge of foam jet from within. It's unsettling, and some primitive survival mechanism inside you tells you the purge must stop. You start thinking about electrolytes, dehydration, that time you drank two cups of Smooth Move tea to drop a few pounds before a wrestling match.

At the same time, even though this process hurts a little, it is preferred to feeling nothing at all. Sure, when you get right down to it, everything you feel is just shit and stardust, or maybe shit feeding stardust. But after feeling empty for so long, it's just nice to feel.

NINE
HUNGRY MOTHER EARTH

YOU wake the next morning, half expecting to be frozen to the ground. Instead, you find yourself tucked into bed. You stretch, feel the sweat-soaked sheets run against the grain of your leg hair. You're naked. You open your eyes, sit up, and feel something give at your waistline. It sounds like Velcro. You tear the sheets away and note the bulging adult diaper unfastened on one side. You feel violated.

"I had to use a diaper, otherwise the room would be covered with Siddhartha's reward."

You open your eyes. "Gary!?"

"Please don't be mad, dude. I swear I never fucked Beth."

You point to your diaper. "I have some higher-order concerns!"

"Bob gave me the diapers. He said they'd help."

You sit up. "How'd you get wrapped up in this shit?"

"That kid I wanted you to meet? He got me into this forum online. It's a group of local kids trying to tie all the conspiracy theories throughout history together. Mandela Effect, Dark factory night shifts at Super Center, Nibiru, The Thule, everything. Bob was one of the administrators."

"How'd you become choleric? Did he suck your dick too?"

"What?!"

"I was just wondering," you try to think up some excuse without fully coming clean, "if it was one of those gay cult things."

"Um, not that I know of." He looks at you quizzically. "I don't think we have a choice to be in or out. We're negatively polarized and the condition just sort of manifests."

"You the one who roped me into this shit?!"

Gary looks down. "No."

You grab him by the shoulders. "What'd you do?!"

"I just showed them the videos. Those scotch-tape edits looked like chaos. I thought you were the enemy."

"I was trying to save people!"

"I know you're on our side now." He steps out of your reach. "I'm sorry."

"It's alright." You try to refasten your diaper. "You're still circulating those videos, right?"

Gary nods.

Your conversation's interrupted by a knock at the door. "Milton! Open the fuck up!"

You jump to your feet. "Did the kids see you come in?"

"They're asleep."

"Good." You push Gary. "Get under the bed!"

"Why?"

"Just hide!"

Gary rolls under the bed and curls into a fetal position.

"Goddamn it!" Another knock at the door. "Tommy! Open the door!"

You hear the toilet lid slam down in the bathroom.

You peer in. "Karen, can you get the door for Daddy while he gets dressed?"

No response.

"Karen?"

"Ack!"

"Karen, are you okay?"

Karen peers in from the living area. "I'm fine, Daddy."

"Where's Tommy?"

"He's on the couch."

"Could you get the door?"

Karen nods and runs to the main entrance.

A familiar cackle resonates from behind the bathroom door. "Ack!"

You open the door quickly to find that fucking vulture perched on your sink, knocking prescription bottles onto your floor.

"Goddamn it, bird!"

The vulture responds with a dry, throaty cough. It tears another bottle out of your medicine cabinet and tosses it haphazardly to the floor. Its contents scatter.

You swat at the bird. "Get out of there!"

It looks straight at you and scatters a few more bottles across the floor with its beak.

"Dude! Knock it off!"

"Who's in there with you?" Beth rips the bathroom door open behind you. Her raised eyebrows and slack-jawed countenance relay the picturesque setting before her. For a brief moment, you see yourself reflected in her expression. There you are, a full-grown man in an adult diaper unhinged on one side, sliding down your leg. Pink foam bubbles from the tub onto the floor as you battle with a vulture destroying your medicine cabinet.

"What the fuck?"

The vulture tosses a bottle of ibuprofen to the floor.

"My thoughts exactly." You swat at the bird.

It flies into the shower, knocking shampoo bottles into the pink foam below.

"Christ. I was hoping to take a shower here. Water's off at our place again, but I can see you're busy."

"Can't you take a shower at Gary's?"

Beth shakes her head. "He's not answering his phone."

You look at the mess on the floor. "I can clean this up for you real quick. You're free to use the shower."

Beth scoops a handful of foam out of the tub and smells it. "Shopping at Lush now?"

You re-fasten your diaper and crouch down to clean out the tub. "Yeah. Sure."

She gently kicks your padded ass. "What's with the diaper?"

"Wild night. I honestly don't know what happened, but I'm not sore or anything, so I think it was just a prank."

"Sore? What kinds of friends are you hanging out with, that your mind goes there?"

"I'm just saying, I don't think anything kinky happened."

Beth takes her shirt off. "If you think I'm going to wipe your ass while you suck your thumb, you've got another thing coming."

"Look," you give up on the pink foam and start cleaning up the pills on the floor. "I'm not trying to seduce you into some weird fetish. I liked the foot thing. I didn't mind the cruelty, but I get it. It's over. It hurts, but I'll be alright."

She takes her pants off. She's wearing no panties.

You rocket to life so furiously your diaper snaps off, dangling from your erection.

You both just stand there, Beth with her trimmed bush and you with a diaper hanging off your cock.

The vulture swoops down and tries to perch on your dick, which is about six inches too small to perch on. It sinks its claws into the diaper as it struggles to get its footing. You slap it until it flies away, diaper in tow.

Beth backs into the shower and smiles. "Come on."

You step in after her, stone faced, afraid that if you act too enthusiastic she'll kick you out.

She kneels down and begins working your shaft. Then she tugs you down to the floor of the tub. She leans back into the foam, and it congeals, cradling the two of you. "This soap is fucking weird."

She puts her arms around your neck and lifts her pelvis to meet your manhood. It is so soft. You enter, find yourself an inch inside . . . and you cum before you're balls deep. You fall into her, struggling against the foam to pull out.

She laughs. "Don't worry, I'm on birth control."

You relax. "When?"

"A couple weeks ago."

You fall onto her completely, spasm rhythmically to a silent stillness. "That was fucking awesome," you remark. Then you notice Gary, watching from under the bed. You gesture for him to leave, mouthing, "Go."

"Kids," he mouths.

"Sorry," you mouth as you push the bathroom door shut.

She holds you there, arms still around your neck. "Will you go down on me?"

You answer by sliding down to meet her vulva. Her natural musk melds with the strong scent of roses until one bouquet becomes indistinguishable from the other, and you bury your face into it. She pushes your mouth into her body and squirms. Soon she bucks and thrashes in the foam. Her clitoris expands to fill your mouth. Then she sighs and deflates. The foam begins to loosen its grip on the two of you. The evidence of your love slides slowly down the drain.

Beth sits up. "Alright. Get off me."

You stand up and help her to her feet.

She turns on the shower water, takes a handful of the foam in the tub, and massages it into her scalp. "I can't get over how good this smells."

You scoop some up and scrub yourself clean. "It is pretty amazing." You step into the water and rinse off. You're skin to skin and erect again. You look up. She's non-responsive. "I better check on the kids," you say.

She bends over and pushes her ass into you. "Let me take care of that first."

Ten minutes later, you step out of the shower feeling not like a new man, but simply feeling like a man again. You wrap your waist in a towel and head into the living area. Karen and Tommy are curled up on the far corner of the couch, watching that fucking bird dig through the cabinets.

"Hey, fucko!"

The bird continues shuffling through the cupboards.

"Get out of there. You're scaring the kids."

The bird dives into the cupboard, grasping at something with its beak.

Karen covers her head with an old throw your mother gave you. "I don't like it."

A few seconds later, the bird falls onto the countertop with a bottle of cough syrup in its mouth. It sets the bottle upright, holds the base with its claws, unscrews the top with its beak, and tips the bottle back.

Karen slowly lowers the blanket.

The vulture empties the bottle into its gullet and drops the bottle. It shakes its head, cranes its neck, and falls to the floor.

You walk behind the counter. The bird is unconscious. You take him into your arms. "Tommy, get the door."

You walk to the open door and gently drop the bird onto the welcome mat. You close and lock the door behind you. "Fucking bird."

Karen drops her blanket and runs into the kitchen. "I'm hungry."

Beth steps out of the bedroom. "I'll make something quick, then we're heading out. What do you want?"

"PB&J!" she screams.

Beth heads for the kitchenette. "You want one too, Tommy?"

He nods, fixated on his game.

You watch her behind the counter, digging in the fridge for the jar of preserves. This is exactly how it was before she left. Exactly as it should be.

She places the jar on the counter. "What the fuck are you staring at?"

You smile. "Just you."

She reaches into the cupboard to grab the peanut butter. She pulls it down and stares at the container. "You know, that jar I brought home the other day, I could have sworn it said Jiffy on it, but when I got back to my place, it was a jar of Jif. You fucking with me?"

You shake your head. "Same thing happened to me. I bought two jars of Jif at the store and when I got home, fucking Jiffy in the bag."

"You mind if I take this one?"

Fuck it, you're working now. "No. Go ahead."

She eyes you suspiciously as she spreads jelly across the bread.

You laugh. "I'm *not* fucking with you!"

She slices the sandwich in half. "You want the crust?" she asks Karen.

Karen takes the plate and skips into the living area. "I'll eat around it."

While Beth makes Tommy's sandwich you do a quick inventory of the bags your kids came with. "You kids got all your shit together?"

They nod.

"Even your dirty clothes? You bag them up?" you ask.

They nod again.

Karen stuffs her mouth full with half a sandwich and turns on the television, coating your remote with jelly.

Beth slides a plate onto the coffee table for Tommy. When he doesn't notice, she gently closes his hand held system and tucks it into her pocket. "Eat. Then we have to go."

You watch Beth strut into the bathroom to grab a brush. She runs it through Karen's hair a few times and tosses it onto the table. "Thanks for letting me shower."

"You're always welcome," you say. And you mean it with every inch of your being.

"Yeah, well. Water's supposed to be back on this afternoon." She stands up. "Come on, kids."

Reluctantly, they slip into their boots and throw their coats on. Beth hands Tommy his 3DS and grabs the Jiffy off the counter. Beth holds up the jar of peanut butter. "Thanks. See you around."

"Bye, kids!"

"Bye, Daddy!"

As they walk through the doorway, Beth screams.

Karen turns to you. The larva is back.

Beth tears it from Karen's forehead. "What is that?!" She kneels and smashes it with the jar of peanut butter until the larva is a smear on the carpet and a rainbow of bilious colors on the wall and the kids' pants. Beth stares at the stain on the floor. "Where did that come from?!" Then she notices the jar of peanut butter, now reading "Jif."

"You switched it?" she asks. "It was in my hands the whole time."

She steps through the doorway to show you. When she holds it up, it reads "Jiffy" again.

"Hang on." You head for the door and slowly pull the welcome mat, now covered with larva innards, into the apartment. As you pull it across the threshold, all traces of the larva disappear. You look at Beth and the kids. "You see that?"

Karen starts to cry.

You push the welcome mat back into the hallway. The guts reappear.

Beth leans over the entrails. "What the fuck is going on?"

"I don't know. Things change when they come into the apartment." Your diagnosis is almost as disappointing as the time you took Tommy to the doctor for a cough and their final report read: "Cough. No course of action suggested." That was $120 well spent . . .

Beth reaches over the threshold with the peanut butter. The jar reads "Jif" as soon as it crosses the barrier between your doorway and the outside world. "No shit, Sherlock. But why is it happening?"

"I don't fucking know."

Karen kicks at the welcome mat. "Put it inside, Daddy. I don't want to look at it."

You drag the mat back into the apartment. The larva remnants disappear again.

"Guess there's no point in trying to prove my brother wrong." Beth sets the peanut butter on the edge of your couch and steps through the doorway. "If you figure out what's going on, let us know."

You watch her step into the hallway, expecting her to change. You seem to recall her hair being dark, and much shorter. But it isn't just the hair you expect to change. You hope, as she crosses that threshold, that she'll realize she's still in love with you. She turns back to look at you. Her hair is shoulder length, blond, pulled back on one side with a small green barrette.

Her hair does not change.

She does not love you.

"Bye, guys."

"Bye," Beth mutters. The kids wave.

You watch them descend the stairs, and then push the welcome mat back out into the hallway with your foot, watching the blood-stains reappear.

You hear Gary crawl out from under your bed and walk into the living area. "What the fuck is that?"

You pull the welcome mat over the threshold. The blood disappears. "I don't know. I think it has something to do with us though."

You close the door and look at the jar of peanut butter on the couch. "Things keep changing when I bring them into my apartment."

You take the Jiffy on the couch and carry it to your doorstep.

It becomes Jif.

Gary grabs the jar, as if seeing the transition isn't enough. He has to feel it. He pulls it into the apartment.

Jiffy.

He pushes it back outside.

Jif.

"That's fucked."

"I'm starting to wonder how many other things would change if I took them across that doorstep."

You walk into the kitchen, resolve to start with something small. The jelly. You decide to start with the jelly.

You carry it to the doorway and walk through. Nothing.

"Well, Raspberry Smuckers is still Raspberry Smuckers." You head back to the fridge, jelly in hand.

Ghost Bob floats in from the bedroom. "Hey," he sighs.

You place the jelly back in the fridge. "What's up?"

"Emergency meeting. Can you guys get to the bridge in ten?"

You throw on your coat. "Sure, as long as I don't fucking disappear when I walk through the doorway."

"What?"

"Nevermind." You grab your keys and head for the door. "You coming, Gary?"

"Let me get my shoes."

In the driveway, the fucking vulture rips through the dumpster.

"Bird, come on!" you shout without looking back.

From the dumpster's innards, the vulture emerges, a black bag of trash in his beak. Crushed soda cans, wilted lettuce, and coffee grounds scatter on the pavement.

Soda cans? It's 2017. Who the fuck doesn't recycle in the twenty-first century?

You keep walking. "You're cleaning that up."

The vulture gargles pink foam in its throat and coughs onto the pavement. It sniffs at the pile and waddles to your side.

The sky is dark, abuzz with flies. They swarm, a morning commute toward the bloated cattle in the distance. How many fucking managers does a Super Center need, anyway?

Enough to bury the sun behind a cascade of translucent wings and black bodies.

The vulture looks up and scrambles for the bridge.

You chalk it up to instinct, but then remember vultures usually flock to flies. Where there are flies there is death. Where there is death, there is a meal. You wonder if the fucking bird knows something you don't know. Then you wonder why you have no recollection of the sky, blackened by man-sized chamber flies.

You'd like to pack up the sky and carry it, box-by-box, into your apartment, see if those flies are the peanut butter sky's missing syllable, the Jif sky's "fy," as it were.

The vulture seems to wave you on with its beak as it hops below. You keep your head up, watching the last of management fly overhead, listening to the unsteady drone like helicopters from a war you never fought in.

The sun returns, rolling across the oily blue coverlet it calls home.

You follow the vulture to the riverside.

Dave sits on a milk crate, digging the toe of his Super Center runners into the earth below. "It's hungry," he says.

"The bird?" you ask.

"The earth." He points down. "We've run dry."

"So I'm not going to shit anymore?" You smile. "Our job is done?"

"No." Dave cracks his knuckles. "We're out of tune with our temperaments." He points to the vulture. "The fucking bird is tightly wound as all hell."

Gary pipes in. "He's just strung out on Tussin. I can't afford his habit anymore. He's up to six bottles a day."

"Gary's apathetic." Dave bows his head. "I'm depressed as fuck."

You shrug. "I feel great."

"That's part of the problem. You're supposed to be melancholic, you black bile fucker!" Dave braces your shoulders and shakes you.

"Sorry?"

He softens his grip. "Look. One of us needs to return to our natural state. I'm not going to get out of this funk until shit gets back to normal. Gary over there can't get his groove back. The bird needs to detox. We need you to get melancholic."

"Christ, I haven't been happy in ages. Why couldn't you guys have come to me just after my wife split up with me? I would have had enough sadness to fuel us for eons."

"We had Bob then."

"I don't know how to make myself sad," you say. "It just happens."

Gary laughs. "Want my job? It'll depress the hell out of you."

"I pretend to work in a dark factory. My job is plenty depressing." As you say this, something drops in the pit of your stomach. Your innards churn audibly.

"That!" Dave points to your stomach. "That's working! What else do you hate about your job?"

"That's about it. It's cold. It's dark. It's fucking boring."

Your stomach growls.

Dave nods. "Yes. Yes?"

"My boss is a fly. He vomited my friend to death."

"Sure. Sure. Keep going!"

"That's it."

Dave plops onto his stump and slumps over.

"What about your ex?" Gary asks.

"Things are going well."

"Yeah, well. I fucked her."

"What?!"

"Yeah. She was . . . she was a choice piece."

Ghost Bob looks at Gary in disbelief, mouths, "That's low, man."

Gary shrugs. "Low?! She's my girlfriend. He just fucked her right in front of me!"

Ghost Bob ghosts his head. "Jesus, you two are fucked up."

"It wasn't as bad as I thought. She had a better time with me. She was like," he pauses to think, "oooh . . . baby. Give me that d-dick."

"You're full of shit, Gary."

"You're not. Christ, look at you. You had two jobs, Milton. Keep your ex happy and shit your pants. Your wife left you, so you're down to one job. One thing expected of you, and you can't even do that. You can't even complete a basic human function."

"Fuck you, Gary. You rent porn to registered sex offenders on welfare central and barf into a burning barrel with a gang of derelict fuckwits under the local bridge. Who are you to talk!?"

"I'm supposed to be cheery, guys. So if you could keep me out of this," Dave mumbles.

Gary stands up. "I'm only twenty-four! I'm going to state school!"

"Spoiler alert, motherfucker. Your job prospects are shit. You're going to be trapped in this shit hole town for the rest of your life, just like me!"

Gary leans into your face. He screams, emphasizing his words awkwardly like an incompetent comic book letterer. "Oh, *the* town is full of shit? Maybe you ought to get . . . *pooping* lessons from the fuckers who *fill* it. You could learn how to poop in your widdle *diapey*. You . . . *fart* . . . fucker!"

"So I ought to talk to your mom, then?"

"You . . . You uuuuuggghhhhllllcccchhh!" Gary barfs onto the ground.

Dave quickly rolls the base of the burning barrel toward Gary. "Into the barrel! Into the barrel!"

Gary leans into the barrel and vomits some more. He props himself up against the edge and wipes the foam from his chin. "Your kids are ugly."

That. That is the final straw that breaks the camel's back. You feel a surge along your lifeline. The foam cascades down your chest. It bubbles up and out of your pants. It climbs up your back like English ivy before falling to the ground.

"You did it, guys!" You hear Dave's voice, but your red rage renders you dumb, deaf, and blind. You dive for Giga Video Gary. The two of you plummet to the ground, topping one another as you roll in half circles, leaving a trail of pink foam in your wake.

Gary rolls you onto your back. His screams transition to thick waves of foam as he vomits onto your face like you're in some grim rendition of a Jerry Springer fetish episode.

Foam shoots from your ears in response. "Don't you ever talk about my kids!"

"Sorry! I'm just trying to save the planet!"

You roll onto Gary and pin his shoulders. "Not my kids."

Gary struggles to get free, then relaxes. "I'm sorry. That was too far."

Dave agrees. "If we're going to be a team, we have to respect one another's boundaries. Milton, it is important you try to sustain this state of misery. And Gary, you must remain enthusiastic. Embrace this passion you feel and work with it. You two may prove our salvation."

Gary sits up. "What about the fucking bird?"

"I'll take him tonight," you say between heavy breaths. "Ought to create an appropriately dismal atmosphere."

Dave reaches into his pocket and hands you a twenty. "Get him two bottles of Maximum Strength Robitussin DM."

"Come on, you fucking bird!"

The vulture waddles to your side.

You take Dave's twenty and pocket it. "We good?"

"We're good." Gary pauses to catch his breath. "Go get your misery on."

TEN
THE FINE ART OF MISERY

FIRST, take your bucket list and burn it. Stagnation coupled with a drive to succeed is the first step to misery. Relegate yourself to feeling trapped. Before, you had dreams that helped promote the illusion of freedom. Now there's no way out, no metaphorical key with which to escape your self-generated prison.

Now your dream of eating chocolate-bacon beaver tails in Ottawa is dead, and with it the legal three-way with sex workers in Canada. But mostly the chocolate-bacon beaver tails.

You never really were very good at setting goals for yourself.

Next, replace that bucket list with a list of all the things you have avoided or have tried to avoid, coupled with the reasons you tried to avoid them:

1. Caffeine (hemorrhoids and anxiety)
2. Your ex-wife (anxiety)
3. Donuts (you gained forty pounds from donuts and pizza)
4. Spiders (because they suck)
5. Tree nuts (allergic)
6. Your ex-wife (sexual frustration)

Decide to self-administer exposure therapy. Head over to the Giga Video and buy a box of coffee. Yes. Coffee comes in boxes for some fucking reason. Imagine its innards coated with BPA and other cancer-causing agents. Don't ask if it is a BPA-free box. That will ruin the "ambiance."

Use the word ambiance a lot, because you fucking hate the word ambiance.

Then buy a bag of tree nuts and a box of heart-shaped donuts and carry them into your apartment's basement, where you imagine radon seeping into your orifices while you make coffee donut cereal in a plastic bucket and eat it until you have heart palpitations.

Lie naked on the basement floor while your heart spasms in your chest. Wait for the spiders to crawl across your extremities. Sweat profusely while you eat macadamia nuts. Wait to see if your throat closes up from the tree nuts.

You've outgrown your tree nut allergy. This revelation is superb, except you're trying to be miserable, so the revelation makes you sad, which is good, so macadamia nuts are your bae.

Incorporate the word "bae" into non-sequitur conversations with yourself, because you fucking hate the word bae and you love non-sequitur conversations. Bae will ruin those small moments of happiness.

Bae is your bae.

Pour coffee directly onto your anus when your palpitations stop. If this doesn't keep your heart rate up, run back to the store and buy a pack of non-filter cigarettes.

Smoke half a pack of cigarettes until your asshole starts itching.

Scratch that itch until you see tiny blots of blood on the toilet paper you stick a quarter inch up your ass.

Your hemorrhoid crop is sprouting. You will soon ascend to a new level of misery.

Namaste and fuck the world.

Call your ex-wife and tell her they've delayed your paycheck, so she won't be able to buy weed with your child support. Say it just like that. "Sorry you won't be able to buy weed with my child support."

Then ask her if she'll come over and walk on your back with her running shoes.

If she says yes, stick objects in your butthole until you have a prolapsed anus. Be sure there is an opening at both ends of these objects so the "order foam" or whatever can feed Mother Earth from the dirt floor in your basement. This normally takes time, but you have to act fast. Find an assortment of bottles from the redemption center and start sitting on them. If the force of gravity is too great, set a glass bottle against the wall and push back into it until the bottle is base-deep.

Now the local fetishists will be screaming "rosebud!" like Charles Foster Kane in Citizen Kane.

You weren't planning on making circles in your local fetishist community?

You should. Get that rosebud some mileage. You want that prolapsed anus to be the silverback gorilla of your hometown.

If your wife says no, look at the grainy nude pictures she let you take on your fourth anniversary. Get rock solid.

Then stick objects in your butthole until you have a prolapsed anus.

That idea just sort of sticks.

Next, make a list of all the people, places, and things you love or thoroughly enjoy and the reasons you love or thoroughly enjoy those people, places, and things:

1. Your kids (they bring a sense of peace and comfort)
2. Your ex-wife (when she lets you get within two feet of her)
3. Sex (self-explanatory)
4. The mailman (he's just friendly and restores your faith in humanity) *Note: go back to the "things I hate" list and add "hyperbole" next to "ambiance" and "bae"*
5. Shopping at Super Center with the kids (a sense of peace and comfort)
6. Writing poetry (a sense of accomplishment)

Do not abandon your kids. Your ex-wife makes you just as miserable as she makes you happy, and the happy bits make the miserable parts all the more bitter, so decide to keep fucking her, even though the goal was to remove as many things on this list from your life as possible.

You're left with items 4-6.

You have to shop to stay alive. Of course, starvation would be pretty fucking miserable. So decide to fast.

You don't want to stop writing poetry. You don't want to, so decide instead to infuse the experience with shame, doubt, and self-hatred.

You also need to alienate the mailman.

Resolve to write really awkward love poetry to the mailman.

Poem one should be an ode to the mailman's aging flesh, but the poem helps him transcend that husk with interminable desire for your prolapsed anus:

Desire's Aging Conduit

His flaking flesh does not squelch desire.
Nor does his crow's peak,
Nor the veins protruding from his spindly legs.

He is frail, but finds frailty is a state that,
Against his will,
Affords desire.
Could it be for.
My prolapsed anus?

Pepper poem two with rhyme. That will almost be enough to ruin poetry for you entirely. But the piece de resistance will be your non-sequitur metaphor, your likening of love to a Robitussin-addicted vulture:

My Love is a Tussin Vulture

I look with tired eyes upon the Tussin Vulture, asking,
"What's the difference between love and obsession?
What's the difference between psychosis and affection?"

The Tussin Vulture retches,
takes another pull from his Extra Strength Robitussin DM,
and replies, "Nothing."
It is then that I know love.

FUCK HAPPINESS

My love is a Tussin Vulture,
Digging through your dumpster heart
For his next fix.

Your love is medically-induced sociopathy.
Let me drink the sweet
Dextromethorphan of your heart.

In poem three . . . just title poem three "Bae." The details are ir-relevant.

Bae

You could be my bae.
I send my heart to you in a lackluster package.
Please don't return to sender,
Like you did that time I didn't shovel the snow bank
In front of my mailbox.

I could be your bae.
Your time-worn hands
Would be my unboxing.
Be gentle with my bubble wrap.

Take the three poems and place them gently in your mailbox. You want to put his name on it, but you realize you don't remem-ber his name, so you just write "For You" on the folded paper. Casually place them inside the mailbox, and lift the flag.

Close the mailbox door and realize if you take one step you are going to shit your pants. Your neighbor, Mrs. Hendrick, is check-ing her mail, eyeing you cautiously. She will notice if you shit your-self.

Look back, make sure she's watching.

Take one step.

Shit yourself.

Keep shitting until your pants are soaked, and your ass sounds like a Keurig squeezing out the last few drops of dark blend.

Listen to Mrs. Hendrick gasp in shock, wrestle the newspaper from her mailbox, and limp back inside as fast as possible, as if shitting your pants in public puts her in imminent danger.

Now stop shitting.

Seriously, you have to stop shitting yourself or you'll die.

At least go inside and clean yourself up.

ELEVEN
YOU THINK YOU MAY HAVE
GIVEN BIRTH TO A
DAYCARE FACILITY

AFTER you clean up for work, you settle into bed and fold the sheets up over your neck. You tuck the blanket around your head until only your face remains. You touch yourself and try not to think of the pain throbbing in your groin. You really need to get that checked. If it is cancer . . . no. You can't think about that right now. You only have twenty minutes before work and you need to rub one out of Burnsie.

You dredge up an image of your wife hovering over you. She looks down at your blanket beard and your blanket body. She laughs at the small lump throbbing at the center of your covered mass. She kneels at your side and gathers the blankets around your cock and chews softly on the tip of your member. It reminds you of your friend in high school who used to wrap paper around his thumb and chew it. "It hurts your thumb but feels good on your teeth, so your brain doesn't know what the fuck to do," he explained, chewing. "Try it."

He was right. It was one of the strangest non-sexual sensations you ever felt.

. . . and you grow soft.

Focus.

You try to think back to your wife, but no matter how many comforters she chews your dick through, you can't escape the sting of losing her.

So you revert to one of your favorite fantasies, a sentient ass hanging out of your television set.

On some level, this is how emasculated you have become. You can't fantasize about having sex with a composite female, complete with all facets of a real woman. Instead, you compartmentalize the female body, fetishize the ass, or a pair of tits. You begin to understand why the glory hole is so appealing. It reduces another person to their sex organs. It strips sexual encounters of the stark reality that there's a mind and soul attached to the pecker poking through the hole. That reality is stark because you fear rejection, and therefore connection. At some point during interface, you imagine every person will reach a threshold of connection at which rejection is inevitable. Your marriage suggests your hypothesis is true, and six years is the maximum threshold of connection in your interpersonal relationships.

You close your eyes and tug yourself, thinking about that ass. It backs into you until the entire woman falls through the television onto your floor. You grab her hips and thrust into her. As you begin to cum she moans "Don't care. Child support. You're going to lose your fucking license" in your wife's voice.

Then everything goes black. You're just a series of spasms, flesh jerking itself back to stasis.

When you're done, you open your eyes. You're on the road.

On your way to Super Center.

This situation has grown all too familiar. You know the routine: That part of your mind activates, reminding you, *Hey. You're masturbating. You shouldn't be doing this in public.*

Then you wait a minute for the rest of your brain to catch up, to realize you're not actually jerking off as you walk down the road.

But it never catches up. You are not tucked away in the safety of your comforter. You have, in fact, climaxed yourself to work.

You turn at the small pond and wade through the water, as dark and thick as chocolate milk. You watch the geese bathe themselves in their own filth.

This is not chocolate milk.

The cold water seeps through your pants, gently caresses your butthole. Your ripe, sore butthole. Goose shit bubbles into your orifice as you break shore. You feel yourself empty through the parking lot.

PCK FCE backs into a handicapped space near home and garden, still wearing the green push up bra. She revs her engine at you.

You pretend not to see her.

PCK FCE slowly pulls out of the lot, following you. She honks. You do not turn. You've already passed the main entrance. You're being corralled into home and garden.

You fucking hate home and garden.

PCK FCE stops at the electric doors and honks continuously as you pass the cashier. The walls are lined with wire frame deer adorned with Christmas lights. The display models slowly lower their heads and pick at nothing on the concrete floor. Wire frame Al Bundys toss invisible footballs to their invisible teammates.

The incessant droning of PCK FCE is replaced by the sound of unintelligible voices on your boss' television.

You hear them in the fitness aisle as you pass the dumbbells. "You can spare forty dollars, Milton," they whisper through the haze of hushed tones.

You hear them from the toy aisle. "A pie-eyed gaze, the Da Vinci-esque smirk posted across faces like billboards for the leeches," the cardboard box supermodels tell you.

"The antebellum scene so violet. So graze. And who was it?" you ask them.

They do not respond.

You walk into the rear office to find the unintelligible voices are, in fact, your boss snoring.

"Sir?"

The thought monitor flickers like a strobe light. Your boss' proboscis flops across the desktop as he snores, but you only see its movements in quick flashes as the thought monitor continues to image stutter.

You round the desk to see who or what the monitor is picking up on tonight.

Please don't be Mom, you think, reminding yourself it could be worse. You revise your mantra. *Please don't be Mom naked*, you repeat.

It isn't your mom.

It's your dream.

Center screen there's a cauldron or lake or cauldron and lake. Fog rolls through the surrounding trees toward the edge of the water. You hear the drone of chamber flies.

The cauldron or lake or cauldron and lake has dried up. The fog has dissipated. The flies lick their appendages. In every direction, thousands of . . . it isn't you refracted in black, broken-mirror eyes.

It's your boss.

He's paralyzed. He tries to scream for help, but his mouth is packed with gauze. He flails wildly as the flies envelope him.

You place your hand on his shoulder, eyes still on the screen, and shake him.

On the screen, the chamber flies coat his body in digestive fluids. He melts into the cauldron or lake or cauldron and lake.

Your bowels knot. You drop to your knees. Something knocks at your back door from within. It pushes your brown balloon knot until it threatens to give under the pressure.

You have no choice but to pull down your pants to let this— whatever this is—out. You unzip and tug your pants down to your knees, look up to make sure your boss is still sleeping.

He is no longer sleeping. Instead, all that remains of him is a pile of digestive juices running down the front of the desk. Whatever happened to him on the thought monitor has transposed to reality.

You stare at the ceiling to make sure the chamber flies aren't hovering above you.

There are only crisscrossing rafters below aluminum roofing.

You look down.

There is no cauldron or lake or cauldron and lake beneath you.

But something is still struggling to make its way into this world through you. Your body fights against the movement, but eventually you hear flesh rend and . . . my god, did you just hear your bones shifting? Which bones were they?

You look back to see your ass split like a halved coconut and a viscous heap of flowery universe purity desk high that presumably just came out of you.

You study the heap carefully. It pulses rhythmically.

Inside, something stirs. You reach in slowly. Your hand moves through the outer layers like a spoon through Jell-o until you feel a warm fluid center. You slide your other hand in and tear at the gelatin-like substance until you uncover the contents within.

It's a man.

It's a man in your boss' clothes.

It is a man in your boss' clothes, snoring like your boss.

You brush the . . . male version of amniotic fluid—you don't know what the fuck it is—away from your human boss' face and study him carefully. He looks to be middle-aged, portly, and balding. His hand is tucked firmly into his pants.

He is Al Bundy.

You want to shake his hand.

You want his autograph, but the shift clock is about to start and you need to punch in, so you lift Al Bundy into his seat behind the desk and prop him upright. His head hangs over the back of the seat, which is optimal because you need to clean the desk off or put something down so Al Bundy's face doesn't melt off when he leans forward. You grab a stack of magazines from the filing cabinet behind the desk and lay them across the front of the desk. You lean Al Bundy forward onto a pile of glossy paper tits, grab your dolly, and head out to automotive.

Silence.

You've only been working a short while, and already you're beginning to feel like such a light load isn't quite enough. You'd always convinced yourself you wanted to do nothing when you got older, but like many, the best compromise is doing nothing under the façade of doing something.

You sit in an office for forty hours a week, doing as close to nothing as possible.

You traipse through the aisles of a Super Center for thirty hours a week, doing as close to nothing as possible.

You talk about how hard you work, and after a while you're not sure whether you're trying to convince yourself or the people around you that you work hard.

Either way, nobody fucking believes it.

For years you convinced yourself that pregnancy was the easiest way to do something while doing nothing. You just sit there on autopilot and this living being grows inside you. All you have to do is eat, which most people love, and suddenly a baby arrives.

But after giving birth to your boss, you're starting to realize you were wrong. Giving birth is a nightmare.

Then you remember your wife's swollen feet, her 'special diet' the doctor forced her to go on to avoid gestational diabetes, or how you used to get so drunk that you couldn't even walk to the store across the road to pick up the weird ass food she was craving. Carrying the child to term was a pain in the ass as well.

The only fun part about pregnancy is the sex, and you're starting to suspect you weren't very good at that either.

You remember one of your professors talking about how women create and men destroy, that at the core of gender were two phallic symbols defining our perception of reality. Men viewed the world through a phallic kaleidoscope while women viewed the world through rose-tinted labia.

As such, men saw themselves as an extension of their genitals. They built monuments to their genitals. Any object on the planet they could not fuck, they created tools to smash and bore orifices into until they could fuck it.

Women, on the other hand, took the entire world into their womb, attempting to nurture, to heal the bruised egos of men whose tiny members would never be large or hard enough to smash through their innately bruised egos.

Women, with a womb-like capacity for caring that expanded far beyond any man's ability to single-handedly fill that vast expanse.

In sum: men are dicks.

But women, women are so much more.

FUCK HAPPINESS

For the first time in your life, you're learning to embrace this. Partially because you watched your wife become a mother. Partially because you have watched your daughter grow. Finally, because you just pushed a full grown man out of your ham flower.

You wonder if, as a result of giving birth, you're any less prone to wanting to smash the world with phallic extensions of the self. You go back to your earliest memories of wanting to meet existence with blunt-force trauma, in part because you're bored, in part because any reflection on the past will bring you misery.

When you were a child you wanted to destroy any and all living things smaller than yourself. You can't remember if it was learned or primal. It was certainly naturalized.

People always frame things in a context they can understand. Killing is natural. Men like to hunt things. Men like to kill things. Own things. So when you gave the dead bird to the neighbor girl as a birthday gift, her parents laughed it off. Boys will be boys, after all.

So when you got bitten by the red ants in the front yard and got caught with a pack of matches burning them as they crawled out of their ant hill, you got in trouble for stealing matches. But killing the ants, that was fine.

Killing. That was normal.

A few years later your neighbor gave you a dollar apiece for each garter snake you killed in his yard. You and the neighbor kid traipsed through the grass with golf clubs, rushing them out of the grass and beating them.

You got three dollars that day.

Killing. That was normal. Killing pays, even.

You remember the first time you felt guilty about killing. Your dad found a snake in the front yard. He held it underfoot and told you to get your BB gun, the two-pump gun that looked like an AR-15 but was so weak it wouldn't shoot all the way through a bull frog like your cousin's pellet gun. You grabbed your gun and brought it out. Your dad lifted his boot. The snake was blind, both eyes steel and lifeless like cartoon characters from the '20s. You stood in your father's shadow, like you did the first time you shot a gun. Your shoulder bruised. That thunder-clap sound still resonates outside your bedroom window on weekends. You still hear people in your town killing or training to kill. You cried because the recoil hurt.

But the killing was normal.

Killing doesn't hurt. You taught yourself that. You compartmentalize the aspects of killing that hurt in the same way you compartmentalize and fetishize the female body. Those steel eyes become those stupid fucking eyes and you shoot them first to stop the pain. Then the killing becomes normal again.

And it isn't just you. Everyone's moral parameters work on a sliding scale. You see it on your social media. You see it in military rhetoric. You see it in the way discourse wraps around logic, around our propensity to kill.

Killing, that's wrong. But defending our country, that's okay.

Killing, that's wrong. But the Bible says an eye for an eye.

Killing, that's wrong. But as long as you're not pulling the trigger, it's fine.

Killing, that's wrong, so you deserve to die for doing it.

We're all killers. The means are different but the name of the game is the same. We're all loaded guns. Trigger words. Dagger-like looks. Anything can kill. Anyone can kill. Words, stares, shunning, those are the drones of intellectual warfare, the weapons that kill that we don't have to face the consequence of. Everyday life, that might be the cruelest fucking war, because none of us have to be accountable. We just phase out. We just ghost. We just shut off our fucking newsfeed or disable our social media accounts until shit blows over.

At least phallic monuments to death are cool. You want a giant obelisk hoisted up above your rotting cock, a monument to your genital inadequacy that will far outlive any memory of your shriveled member.

. . . It won't stop you from dying though.

Suddenly, the knot you hadn't even had time to forget returns.

The pressure follows. The veins and flesh in your ass strain like your 32 jeans after six months of beer and pizza. Then they stretch like those same jeans after nine months of beer and pizza.

Your rusted bullet hole bursts like that very same pair of jeans after a year and a half of beer and pizza.

And with your old dirt road, the 36 pants you wear today go, obliterated by yet another goddamned gelatinous mass of materialized order.

This payload is larger, significantly larger, than the last. It towers above you. You have a hard time believing this came out of you, but there it is.

Like before, you reach inside with both hands, but this deposit is more viscous. You lose your footing and slip inside completely.

Once you fall through the outer shell, you find yourself in a carpeted room. At least it feels like carpet. You scrape the order-afterbirth from your eyes and open them. There's no sign of your entrance behind you. No sign of the egg, or whatever the fuck you just fell inside.

You're in a daycare center. Not a bloated eight-ton cow daycare facility, but an honest to goodness daycare facility.

Children's voices echo through the hallway, but they are nowhere to be found. You walk through the hallways, peer into each room. There are no larvae squirming across the play mats. There are no flies crawling up the walls. There are no humans. The rooms are empty.

You return to the hallway and head for the front doors. The windows are covered with your purity foam. You open the doors, worm through the cascade of foam, and dry your eyes again.

You're in the Super Center parking lot.

The bloated cow facility is gone, replaced by brick and mortar.

You think you may have given birth to a daycare facility.

PCK FCE still waits for you near home and garden. Super Center security at some point has left you several warning notices. PCK FCE's tires are covered with chalk lines, one for every damned ticket on the windshield.

She doesn't start.

You fumble through your keys and turn the key in the ignition. The engine purrs like PCK FCE did the first time you met her. But back then, you didn't have to turn the key to get her engines roaring.

It just happened.

Even though you've only known PCK FCE a few days, she's a familiar element of a world changing too fast for you to keep up with. PCK FCE is changing too, but PCK FCE is still PCK FCE. PCK FCE still gets you from point a to point b.

You roll into your driveway that morning, despondent, broken. Grieving the world you know, wondering if you grieved for and forgot the world you knew before.

You wonder if you shit jars of Jiffy onto the Super Center shelves when things changed the first time.

The only changes you remembered then—peanut butter, your wife's hairstyle, Berenstein Bears—those were all superficial. Now to restore those superficial memories of some alternate reality, people and places you know now are changing, and it all seems wrong.

You slide into bed without showering and watch the digital clock cast shadows across your bedspread. You reach into the top drawer of your nightstand and clutch a fistful of Burger King napkins.

You touch yourself until you're half hard, but you can't shake your sense of loss. PCK FCE isn't sentient, and her tits look smaller than they used to.

And that daycare carcass was starting to grow on you.

The one consolation is that your cock still goes soft when you find yourself distracted in thought.

You're still too introspective to masturbate.

So that's something.

TWELVE
SOUL SECRETIONS

YOU wake the next morning to the sound of children. Your children. Beth hammers on the front door. "Goddamn it, Milton!"

"Coming!" You sit up and find yourself wrapped in the thick froth of your innards.

The pounding continues.

You feel your way to the window, fumble with the lock, and open it. You begin cupping the foam and shoveling it out the window with your hands. The bubbles pop from your frantic movements. This effort is futile. Your place is filled with flower foam, and there's nothing you can do about it.

"Come on, Milton!"

"Hang on! I'm getting dressed!"

"Like I haven't seen you naked before! Hurry the fuck up!"

You make it to your bedroom door, pull it open, and sigh in relief. At least the fucking mess is contained.

You slam the bedroom door shut behind you and open the main entrance.

Beth storms in. "About fucking time."

The kids follow behind her.

"Hi, Daddy."

"Hi, Dad."

"Hey, kids. How, uh. How's it going?"

They plop down on the couch. "Good."

Beth darts straight for the bedroom door. "What you hiding?"

"Leave that closed, please."

She smiles. "You got someone in there?" Before you can answer, she turns the knob and shoulders the door open.

Karen sees the foam at the door and runs into the bedroom. "Bubble bath!" she screams.

"No, no." You grab Karen by the arm. "It's not a bubble bath."

Karen scoops a handful out of the opening. "It smells like flowers."

Beth reaches into the foam. "What happened?"

"I have no fucking idea."

"You're going to get water damage."

"I'm trying to clean it out. I've got the window open."

Beth heads for the kitchenette. "You got any cardboard around here."

"In the recycle bin downstairs."

"Go grab some, like larger sheets. Case of beer sized. We can scoop and push it out the window that way."

"What if the landlord sees?" you ask.

"You've got to do something with the shit, Milton."

You nod submissively and head downstairs.

How the fuck are you going to live without her? You already know the answer. You'll scoop the wreck your life has become out of your window one handful at a time when a bowl, a sheet of cardboard, or just about fucking anything would work more effectively. But you'll be too stupid and frantic to realize because Beth isn't there to kick you in the ass.

You open the dumpster lid, grab a few broken down shipping boxes, and run them upstairs.

Beth meets you at the door. She grabs one of the flattened shipping boxes and heads for your bedroom. "You're an idiot, Milton."

You follow. "It isn't my fault."

"What happened? You fall asleep with the shower running?"

"No, I—"

Beth scoops the foam from the floor and pushes it up and out the window. "Don't bullshit me, Milton. What is this shit and why is there so much of it?"

"It's," you stop. "It's coming out of me."

"What do you mean it's coming out of you? Are you burping that shit up? Christ, maybe you ought to talk to a doctor, get a different antacid prescription or something."

"Maybe."

"So this . . . all of this came out of you?"

You nod.

"Like vomit, burping, what?"

"You're going to be pissed."

"Tell me, fuckhead."

"It comes out wherever it can. My ears, eyes . . . my ass."

"What!?"

"I'm sorry."

"Christ!" Beth spits and wipes her face. "Some of that shit got in my mouth!" She beats you with her cardboard shovel. "What the fuck is wrong with you!?"

Karen runs up to the edge of the doorway. "Look Mom, I made a beard!"

"Get that shit off your face, Karen!"

Karen walks away, head lowered.

Beth glares at you, gives you one more good smack on the head and shoulders before continuing to shovel your harmony sauce out the window. "God I hate you sometimes."

You shovel beside her. "It isn't like I can control it."

"We fucked in that, Milton. I washed my hair with it."

"I did too."

"It really came out of your ass?"

"Some of it, yes. I'm sorry."

"God. Are you okay? I mean, do you feel okay?"

"I feel fine."

"Do you have any idea what's causing it?"

"It's—it's got something to do with the peanut butter jars, and the flies at Super Center."

"Don't start with that non-sequitur bullshit. Ooh, the reciprocal copula altered, congealed with drops of sweat until the dead sleep," she mutters in a mocking tone. "Fuck off."

"I'm serious. Haven't you noticed things have been a little fucked up lately?"

"Everything's been fucked up since you got kicked out of college."

"Not just that. I mean, there are flies working at Super Center."

"Always have been."

"I'm not so sure. I think things have been changing. Whatever's causing it is changing our consciousness as well, or our memories. Something. But there are little things we do notice, like the peanut butter, or your hair."

"And how does" —she waves around the room— "this figure into that?"

You catch yourself. You trust her, but you don't want to tell her about the cult of four temperaments. "All I know is, the more this shit comes out of me, the more things seem to revert back to normal." You wait for her reaction. She just keeps shoveling. "My boss at Super Center, he's human now."

She just keeps shoveling.

"You don't believe me?"

"I don't know what to think. Shit's definitely been weird lately. That fucking maggot on Karen's head. The Jif thing is weird. I brought the jar back today, by the way. I just want to see it again. I'm starting to think I'm going insane. What if whatever's wrong with you is infectious, like you used to say? What if me and the kids have it too?"

"I don't think this is contagious."

"What if we start shitting foam and talking word salad to everyone in town? They'll lock all of us away." She tears up. "If my kids get sick I swear, Milton. I'll fucking kill you."

"They're not going to get sick. Trust me. Things are getting better. They're changing."

"Will you at least go to the doctor, get this shit checked out?"

"I suppose I could."

"Do. Nobody should be shitting roomfuls of . . . whatever this pink stuff is. You say things are changing back to normal. Look around you. *This* is not normal."

Together, you've cleared out most of the room. The foam now sits knee high. "We're a pretty good team, aren't we?"

She stands up straight, winded. "This wasn't how I planned to spend my morning."

You stand over her, wipe a small dollop of foam from her cheek. You lean in to kiss her.

She stops you, but doesn't pull away. "No. I'm sorry."

"But last time—"

"—was fun, yes. I enjoyed it. But it was just a heat of the moment kind of thing."

"So you're never going to let me touch you again?"

"I'm not going to say never again, but not today. Okay?"

You try to smile. "Sure."

She gently takes your arms off her waist. "Alright. I'm heading out. You got the kids for a bit, alright?"

"Okay?"

"We talked about this!"

You stare at her, perplexed.

"I take it you never dug out the birth certificates for me either, then?"

"Birth certificates?"

"Fuck!" She paces the floor. "I'm applying for a new job and I'm going to need them to get the kids insurance."

"So you're going to go for full custody?"

"No. But I am going to be their primary caregiver. We talked about this too. Goddamn it, Milton."

"I honestly don't remember this conversation. Maybe you think we talked about this, but our reality has altered."

"Maybe you're a forgetful fuck, Milton. Why can't *that* change?" Beth walks into the neighboring room. "Tom, where's your bag?"

You follow. "What's up?"

Beth pulls the jar of Jiffy out of Tom's backpack. She turns it over in her hands. "I still don't believe it." She walks to your doorway and holds the jar outward through the threshold.

Jif.

She pulls the jar back in, studies the list of ingredients, the factory location, everything. "I wonder if it's just the name that changes." She holds it outside again. "Lexington, Kentucky inside. Lexington, Kentucky outside." She cradles the jar inside your apartment. "Ingredients are the same too. It's just the name. Weird." She sets the jar down on your kitchenette counter. "You really think that shit coming out of your ass is doing this?"

Tommy looks up. "What shit?"

"The pink stuff. In the bedroom," you say.

Karen wipes the remaining beard off her face. "That came out of your butt?!"

Tommy laughs. "You put it on your face."

"Shut up! I didn't know!"

"Butt beard." Tommy continues laughing.

"Shut up!" Karen storms to the sink and rinses her face off.

Beth picks up her purse and heads for the door. "You two be good for your father. And don't put any more of that shit on your face, Karen."

You watch from the window as Beth pulls out of the driveway. "Kids."

They're transfixed by screens aglow with the latest trends.

"Kids?"

Karen stares over her brother's shoulder at Raichu knocking the shit out of Clefairy. "What, Daddy?"

"I have to go . . ." *Think, you bastard, think. If you say you want to go to the store, they'll want to go too.* "I have to go see a friend just a few doors down. You two be alright for a second?"

They nod.

And you're out the door.

You comb your surroundings outside for evidence of change.

There are still six pumps at the gas station adjoining Giga Video.

The pavement is still lined with dried frog corpses from the last rainstorm.

The bridge is still puke green.

FUCK HAPPINESS

The juggalo tags under the bridge are still "4-lyfe."

But it isn't so much what hasn't changed that you're concerned with. On some level, you're hoping certain things, or certain people, *have* changed. Ideally, you're hoping evidence of the cult has disappeared, foreshadowing the inevitable drying up of your bowels.

You hop over the side of the bridge and make your way down to the meeting place. You spot the burning barrel first.

No Dave.

No Ed.

No Ghost Bob.

Bottles of Robitussin roll along the edge of the river while others dot the small islands downstream.

You walk toward them, hopeful these are the last remnants of your foray into the absurdist hero's journey.

Then you see the vulture. Ed. He's grabbing each bottle by the opening and trying to pour the remnants down his throat.

You notice what appears to be a dirty wig blowing nearby.

Dave.

Your heart sinks.

Your pants fill.

The only thing missing is Ghost Bob.

And Gary.

Ed hops up to you and angrily tosses a bottle at you with his beak. "Squak!"

You kick the bottle back at him. "Fuck off, bird."

The dirty wig on the shoreline turns. It turns back toward the water.

"Do you have any way to tell if what we're doing is making any difference?"

Dave watches the water cascade across the rocks. "Nothing quantifiable."

"Have you noticed anything change?"

He shakes his head, still barely acknowledging you.

"I have."

This gets his attention.

"Like what?"

"Daycare center's not a giant cow corpse anymore."

No reaction.

"Over at the Super Center?"

He shakes his head.

"And shit keeps changing in my apartment. My kid came home with a giant maggot on her forehead the other day. When we walked through the door it disappeared. Jif peanut butter becomes Jiffy inside my apartment."

"Things are going to seem strange. They'll likely get worse before they get better."

"Likely? I thought we were taking a calculated risk here. Don't you know what's going to change?"

Dave stands up. "I have a sense of what was. I know we're returning to that state. What we'll lose, or gain, in the process . . . I'm not so sure."

"Why even change it back then?"

"Because this." He opens his hands to the sky. "Well, this looks natural. But the flies, the vulture hooked on Robitussin, those things are not normal."

"Is the bird aware that it might vomit itself out of existence?"

"Either that or he could be returned to his true form. Maybe he was a person before all of this."

"And when he transforms, will the metamorphosis be taking place in my bowels?"

"What?"

"My boss was cannibalized in his dream the other night. After he disintegrated, I gave birth to his human form."

"That's—"

"—Then," you interrupt. "Then I shit out the new daycare facility."

"Your boss. He was a fly?"

"Was. He's human now. Is that normal?"

"I suppose that's a good thing."

"Didn't feel like a good thing at the time." You point to the lacerations running down his arm. "You going to take the brunt of the re-birthing from now on? Bleed a couple shift managers out of those scars?"

He shakes his head. "This has never happened before."

"You obviously have no idea what the fuck is going on. I get that. But what do you *think* all of this means?"

"I think it means things are more out of balance than I thought." He pauses. "Do you remember Tang?"

"What the fuck is Tang?"

"It was a powdered drink when I was a kid. Then it wasn't. It's one of the first small things I noticed. After that, cartoon characters started changing. Their color, their names. Nobody believed me. Then one summer I woke up late, but it was still dark. The skies were black with swarms of flies. I asked my mother what was happening. 'Morning commute,' she replied nonchalantly. Like we'd seen it one hundred times. The next summer, the town my grandmother grew up in and the nearest city merged, like just half of each place and everything between our town and the city was just . . . gone.

"I kept trying to point the changes out to people. Everyone was so disaffected. I thought I was losing it. That's when I decided to end it. I waited until my mother left for work, smashed a blade out of her razor, and opened myself up in the bathtub. I passed out at the first sight of blood." He smiles. "I woke up six hours later. The bathroom was flooded. Slick with blood. I should have been dead. I didn't stop bleeding for weeks. I was so weak. Then my blood started to thicken. It bubbled to the surface of my wounds. I know it sounds stupid, but that evening when my mom came in to check on me, she brought me a cup of Tang. Tasted like shit, but it was familiar.

"Anyway, the more I . . . foamed, the more smaller things kept returning to normal. But the flies always remained."

"They're leaving now."

Dave leans forward and scoops a handful of sand into his palm. "So it seems."

"Shouldn't you be happy?"

"Should be. I'm wondering how deep this goes. How far we have to go with all of this." Dave breathes deeply. "So Tang, when it came back, I took that as a sign I was on the right track. You know how I knew you were one of us?"

"How?"

Dave reaches into his pocket and pulls out a small packet of Tang. "I carry this wherever I go. It is a dowsing rod for order. Used to be that when I was in a pocket of augmented order the Tang would appear in my pocket." He hands it to you. "Now, when I enter a pocket of order, the Tang disappears. What we're doing, it is a process of unraveling. Things reappear, change, and then disappear. Not everything will disappear, but things that never were, they'll be gone forever."

You turn the Tang packet over, study it briefly, and hand it back to him.

He stuffs the packet into his pocket. "You'll find your own dowsing rod. Your Jiffy, perhaps. They'll help you find the bridges between chaos and order."

"We don't have to go through with this. We could just stop, right? You get your Tang. I get to keep my family."

"At this point, I don't think so. And you don't know that your family is going to disappear. That's just paranoid speculation."

"I'm worried about seeing things change that I don't want to see change."

"It isn't so bad. Someone out there remembers the way things were before we became naturalized to the chaos." Dave tosses a pebble into the river. "Imagine how they feel."

"If they're not all dead. This shit didn't happen overnight."

"Even if they're gone, it's the right thing to do, restoring order." Dave stares at the water with black, lifeless eyes. "I'm sorry."

You sit down beside him. "You're gonna be if I have to shit out every employee at Super Center before this is over."

And even though the prospect of birthing the entire world back to its original state makes your entire body feel like white noise, you laugh to dispel the tension.

That evening you resume your work of testing things at the threshold to your apartment. You find a few inconsequential alterations. You sketch up a table and lie down to track the changes:

Product	In Apartment	Outside	Meaning
Lava Bar Soap	Ingredient: Yellow #2 dye	Ingredient: Yellow #5 dye	?
Jif	Product Name: Jiffy	Product Name: Jif	?
Beth	Hair: Blond, shoulder length	Hair: Blond, shoulder length, but it was black at one point.	?

You contemplate the futility of even including a meaning column. At this point you're still in the dark as to what any of this shit means.

You grab your phone and head to the window in your bedroom. You call Giga Video and peer through your curtains as if you're going to be able to see the person on the other end answer.

You still haven't replaced that fucking curtain rod.

The store manager picks up. "Giga Video."

"Gary there?"

"Hang on." He drops the phone on the counter. The rattle is deafening.

You try to figure out how to turn the volume down. There are two buttons, top center. Plus and minus. You push them. Nothing.

You wonder why you still have a landline phone.

The phone rattles on the other end.

"Beth?"

Fucker.

"It's Milton."

"Oh . . . sorry, man."

"It's alright. Look. I need a hand with something. Just another set of eyes. What time you done?"

"I have a few hours left."

"Can you stop by when your shift's up?"

"I—uh, sure."

"Shouldn't take long."

"Alright, man. I'll see you in a while."

"Okay. I'll catch you later."

You hang up.

You head for the door.

You amble out of town, past the water tower, to Super Center.

You walk past the Polk High football field. You climb the chain link fence near Super Center, wade waist deep into the cauldron or lake or cauldron and lake from your dreams. You walk through the bottom of the lake to the other side, over divots in the mountain ranges. Micro-valleys.

At the top of a mountain you notice a red tide beating against the back end of Super Center. The collective figure demands from the razorwash backdrop shutterblindness. Static circling, piling upon inordinate checkerboard pillars, uprooting the barren reds in the distance.

A tree at the edge of the parking lot bears application fruit. You walk inside. The security panels scan you for ID.

The tile becomes a conveyor belt.

You pass the seasonal aisles, head for the ATM.

The ATM wants to know if you would like to check your balance.

You would.

You have $50.00.

You cancel the transaction and grab a basket. You pick up the cheapest shit possible. Juicy Fruit, Big Red, Tic Tacs, Kit Kats, whatever you can get your hands on that's under a dollar.

But you need to diversify. You need more than just candy.

You head to stationary. You buy Bic pens, Ticonderoga #2 pencils, and sticky notes.

You backtrack to the cough medicine and grab a few bottles of Robitussin DM.

You head to the fruit juice, look for the powdered shit. You get Tang.

You head for the peanut butter. You already have Jif. You get Fluff.

Fuck Smuckers.

You already know the jelly hasn't changed.

You head for self-checkout.

You do not get the fucking curtain rod.

You head back over the mountain, through the cauldron or lake or cauldron and lake, down the streets to your home, checking your watch as you go. Gary is almost done with his shift, by your estimation, so you head straight for Giga Video, bags of shit in tow.

He's standing by the edge of the store with Beth. You can hear her cackle from the roadside.

"I got a sitter for tonight, Gary! I already paid her!"

Gary pleads with her. "I'm sorry. Please don't be mad. I can come over later."

You lower your head and turn. You bolt for your apartment.

"Milton!"

Fuck.

You've been spotted.

Beth waves you over. "Come here!"

You walk, head still down, like an obedient dog toward your ex-wife.

She points to the back seat of her car. "Got the kids. Where the fuck were you?"

You hold up your bags. "I had to hit Super Center real quick."

"You couldn't take them with you?"

"It was just a quick trip."

"Karen's too young to be left alone. Get your shit together."

"I'm sorry."

"Why'd you have to go to Super Center? I thought you had work tonight. Why not just go after your shift?"

"Shift was cancelled."

She pops a Newport into her mouth. "You got any plans tonight?"

"No." You look at Gary. Why did you look at Gary? "Yeah."

She inhales deeply. "Well which is it?"

"I've got some things to take care of."

She steps, not toward you but *at* you. "Like what?"

"I'm meeting some friends."

"You don't have any fucking friends, Milton."

Gary takes the cigarette out of Beth's hand and takes a drag. "That's not true."

Beth rips the cigarette out of Gary's hand. "You're defending him?"

You tear the cigarette out of Beth's mouth and throw it on the ground. Fuck this *Lord of the Flies* smoldering conch shell bullshit. You stomp the Newport. "You're not our keeper, Beth."

"Yeah!" Gary adds, recoiling in fear before he even finishes speaking.

Beth steps *at* Gary ominously.

Goddamn she is scary.

She is frightening as all fuck and you want to fuck her.

"Whatever," she resigns. "Fuck you and fuck you too!" She rounds the car, opens her door, and slams it as she falls into the driver seat.

"So I'll see you later then?" Gary asks her.

She rolls down her window and extends her middle finger as she peels out of the Sunoco parking lot.

"I'm fucked." Gary picks up the Newport butt, straightens it, and tries to light it.

You hold your fingers out so Gary will pass you the butt. "She'll get over it."

"You think I should go see her when we're done?"

You take a drag off the butt. When your lungs are full you exhale through your nose and keep sucking until there's nothing left. You toss the butt on the ground. "Are you seriously asking me for relationship advice about my ex-wife?"

"You'd know better than anyone else."

"I'd also be the most likely to lie."

"You still love her?"

You shake your head. "Fucking A, Gary."

"What?"

"Just come on."

When you get to the apartment you dump all the products on your coffee table. "Sit down."

Gary takes a seat on the couch. "What're we doing?"

"We're taking inventory of all the shit that's changed, if any." You slide your chart to him.

"You think all this stuff has changed . . . because of us?"

"I don't know what's changed. I want to get a sense of how far-reaching what's happening is." You pick up the Tic Tacs. "If none of this is different, then maybe we're doing alright. Maybe we have a long way to go before we change something important."

"We want the important things to change."

You take the Tic Tacs to the doorway. "I'm not so sure anymore." You extend your arm across the threshold.

Still Tic Tacs.

You check the ingredients and bring them back across the threshold. Nothing changes. "Remember how the Jif changed when we held it in the hallway? The morning before Karen brought her 'friend' home from daycare. That thing disappeared when we walked through the door. We're not just changing inanimate objects. Living, breathing things are disappearing, or are going to disappear."

"So you think all of this stuff might disappear when you hold it outside?"

You head for the table and scoop all the products into a plastic bag. "No, but you reminded me of something. Some of this stuff might have disappeared once we brought the bags inside." You take the bag to the hallway and set it down. "I just need you to note any changes I tell you about."

Gary takes the paper and lies down near the doorway. "I want to see this shit."

You toss the Tic Tacs on the floor next to him. "Nothing changes there."

You toss the Juicy Fruit over the threshold.

No change.

Big Red: no change.

Ziploc bags: nothing.

You run the Kit Kat bar over the threshold. "Nothing."

"Wait." Gary looks up. "Run it over again."

You slowly push it from the hallway to the living room floor. "Nothing."

"There's a hyphen now."

You pull it into the hallway and push it back into the apartment. "Holy shit."

You toss the Kit Kat bar into a separate pile. This is your Tang. This is one of your dowsing rods. "Write it down."

Gary stares at the candy bar, motionless. "I can't believe that just happened."

"Let's check these pencils."

"Does Dave know about this?"

"Yeah. All along, I suspect."

"Why didn't you tell me?"

"I just did." You toss the pencils across the threshold: nothing. "The question we should be asking is why didn't he tell us."

You pull out the sticky notes and toss them across the threshold: nothing.

Absolutely nothing inside the apartment. You nod at the empty floor where you tossed the sticky notes. "That's what I'm worried about."

"That's what happened to Karen's friend?"

"Well, it was a maggot, but still. How long before something or someone else important disappears?"

"Wait a minute." Gary drops his pencil. "When we came in you let me go first."

"And?"

"What if I would have disappeared?"

"I would have pulled you back across the threshold and you would have been the guy in the hallway."

"It's working." Gary hops to his feet and sets the notebook down on the table. He pulls a vial of ipecac out of his pocket.

You walk through the doorway, close the door behind you. "Don't."

"This is what we wanted."

"This is not what I wanted." You toss the remaining items into the plastic Super Center bag. "I didn't have a choice in any of this. That crap just started oozing out of random orifices one day."

"But you went along with it." Gary uncorks the vial.

"I don't want anyone to get hurt."

"Nobody's going to get hurt." Gary tries to tip the ipecac into his mouth. "Besides, it's only happening in here. Out there things are pretty much the same as they've always been."

You stop his hands, spilling some of the ipecac. "Gary, I think we should stop."

"No." He pulls against your grip and downs the remaining ipecac.

"What about Beth? What if she disappears?"

"Look." Gary wipes the corner of his mouth with his sleeve. "I care about Beth, and I'm not doing this to hurt anybody. But how you feel about losing her . . . I already lost everything I cared about."

He stops, possibly deliberating about whether or not he wants to explain himself. He takes a deep breath. "I keep dreaming about this life I had. It's been the same dreams for years. I was just curious when I started, but now parts of those dreams are real. Floor tile in my house changed the other day. My parents have a deck and a pool now."

"Your parents always had a deck and a pool . . . I think."

Gary shakes his head. "A few months ago they didn't."

"So you're going to risk other people's lives for a few home renovations?"

"It's not just small shit. I think I had a son, Milton. I had a son, and the only time I see him is when I sleep or draw him. It feels so damned real."

"Then you know how I feel. I don't want to lose my kids to this mess."

"I'm sorry." Gary heads for the door. "But if they end up disappearing, then they never were to begin with. Who knows, maybe mine never was to begin with either. There's only one way to find out."

You watch him walk out the door, knowing you could stop him, instead hoping he'll just disappear. You think about chasing him down, or at least making him barf on the concrete roadway so Gary's universe purity won't cause any more shifts, but you don't. Instead, you lie in bed wondering if maybe Gary's right, wondering if maybe this is an out you've never allowed yourself to acknowledge you want.

Either way, you're going to feel conflicted and depressed. If you're looking for an out, there are easier, less-damaging ways to find it. If you're not, then why did you let Gary walk? In some small way, the damning evidence against your venture still doesn't seem real. Even if you knew Gary was going to vomit someone out of existence, you're not sure you could stop him.

You realize that shitting and puking the world to a state of equilibrium is such a passive-aggressive endeavor, which is part of what makes it so easy. You can't confirm whether or not you're *really* making changes. Sure, things are changing, but you can't prove you're the one responsible.

You realize that you, Gary, and Ghost Bob are the perfect people for a cause like this. You're downtrodden enough to want to make a change, but too placated to actively make a change.

You wonder if whatever cosmic entity out there has evolved to facilitate to the current apathy-inducing social virus. This entity, this world, must always have heroes regardless of how they manifest. The age of Ulysses has long passed, replaced by heroes who save the world from the comfort of their couches.

But you, you are the next incarnation of the social justice warrior. Even typing. Even sitting at a computer is too much.

You save the world simply by sustaining your basic functions of survival.

You literally shit and cry the world to its salvation.

But while the effort of today's heroes seems minimal in comparison to those of yore, there is still sacrifice.

There must always be sacrifice.

Therein lies the challenge you're not sure you're willing to accept.

You will not play Abraham, sacrificing your children to a voice that may or may not be there.

You decide it isn't worth thinking about anymore.

You fall asleep wondering if your wife's blond hair is more of a yellow #2 or a yellow #5, and whether or not there might be a correlation.

What color did Dave say Tang was again?

You dream you're in the cauldron or lake or cauldron and lake. Out of the stagnant pool Al Bundy dressed as a fly or a fly dressed as Al Bundy emerges. He speaks in non-sequitur clips of holocaust victims and Bukowski poetry readings.

You watch yourself giving birth to something in the cauldron or lake or cauldron and lake. The foam coalesces with the black stagnant water. Then the roiling subsides. You see a reflection of yourself in the water. Or you under the water. You see your reflection on the surface, and behind your reflection thousands of you refracted in black, broken-mirror eyes.

You just gave birth to your fly self.

Al Bundy dressed as a fly or a fly dressed as Al Bundy addresses you. "The world is self-righting. There are entire species you've never seen whose sustenance depends on imbalance. There's no need for your intervention. If you keep neutralizing your element, you're going to dissipate."

"I didn't choose to be like this."

"Yet here you are, still."

"Tell me how to stop it and I will."

"We can tell you how to stop it, if you tell us how you remember."

Your brows furrow. "What do you mean?"

"As order displaces chaos, your species forgets what order displaces." He pokes your chest with his appendage. "But you remember. Why?"

"I don't know."

"Think! What makes you different?"

"I'm insane?"

Your stomach rumbles. You feel something rise to the surface of your skin. Small teeth bore through your belly button. A writhing maggot stretches through the opening and falls onto the ground.

Al Bundy dressed as a fly or a fly dressed as Al Bundy picks the maggot up. He nods. "You really don't know."

"I'm sorry. I wish I could help." You shrug. "Will you still help me?"

"Stopping is simple, really. Don't be a miserable prick."

"I just found out in the past forty-eight hours that I'm now capable of giving birth to industrial-scale buildings, and that this ability could lead to me shitting everything I love—including myself—out of existence. Kind of hard to keep a cheery disposition."

"You can end it. All you have to do is be happy."

THIRTEEN
THERE IS NO /

YOU wake to the phone by your nightstand.

Beth.

"Milton. Christ, the phone rang for an hour. What's wrong with you?"

"It only rang twice, Beth."

"Whatever." She pauses between phrases to chew whatever the fuck her maw is gnawing on. "The birth certificates. Did you find them?"

"I haven't had a chance to look."

"Hop to it. I'm running down to Mom's tomorrow. I'll be by to pick them up in a bit, alright?"

You roll out of bed and scramble to the kitchenette. "Birth certificates. Birth certificates." You pull the stack of three-ring binders out of one of your cupboards, knowing already they aren't there. You sort through your undergraduate portfolio anyway, half hoping they'll turn up, half reminiscing.

Nothing.

You check under the stack of board games in one of the kitchenette drawers.

You find an ample supply of mouse turds and some loose Candy Land cards. Nothing more.

The fire safe. You know that's where you put them last, but you're afraid to look. Part of you is still quite certain that Beth took them months ago, and this is just another excuse to chastise you for something you didn't do. You know, like fucking *leave her.*

You grab your keys off the counter and rattle through them until you come to the smallest key on the chain. The security this key offers is about equivalent to a fucking paperclip. It's worthless. You doubt the safe would even survive a basic house fire.

Doesn't matter. Open the safe. Pore over the contents.

It's surprisingly vacant, like the black eyes hot glued onto the Rudolph decorations at Super Center. Of two M.A. thesis copies, only one remains. Your printed corpus linguistics studies: gone. Wedding pictures: gone. Birth certificates: gone. All that remains are tax receipts and a chemical hazard manual you got when you dabbled in journalism during your first year in college.

You see the jar of Jiffy on the countertop, and you wonder.

You see the jar of Jiffy on the countertop, and you don't want to know.

Yet you get up off your knees and carry the fire safe over the threshold, into the hallway, and sure as shit the safe is overflowing with paperwork.

Another draft of your M.A. data strains. Wedding pictures, albeit a bit water damaged for some reason. Endless reams of paper filled with coded documents.

. . . The birth certificates.

You pull them out of the fire safe.

You literally shake as you slowly push them over the threshold, into your apartment, and watch them disappear.

You tear them back quickly and cradle them like they're your actual children.

The birth certificates. Here in the hallway.

Gone in your apartment.

Your wedding photos. Here in the hallway.

Gone in the apartment.

These artifacts, these are not your Tang. It was easy to see Tang, or a Kit Kat bar as tools, dowsing rods to find the spaces between chaos and order. But the photos and your kids' birth certificates, these are relics of a dying world that you are wiping out of existence.

Up to this point, you used to laugh at people for missing what they never had. You laughed when your college buddies pooled their money together to buy the original Lego Millennium Falcon because none of them ever got to assemble it as children.

But maybe they had. Maybe in some distant part of their collective consciousness, they remembered spending Christmas morning sorting through gray Lego chips, drinking Tang, and eating Jiffy peanut butter. Maybe, after finishing lunch, they hopped in the shower and scrubbed their bodies with yellow #2 while their blond mothers delicately pinned their hair back with barrettes on one side.

Maybe, years later, they got to keep their Millennium Falcons and their Jiffy. Maybe they mixed their Tang with some non-existent white rum that dulled the pain of remembering the wife and kids they never had.

It hits you in wave after wave at this point.

Your marriage isn't just over. In whatever reality you're shitting into existence, it never was.

And your kids are going to meet the same fate unless you manage to stop crying and shitting all over yourself in the hallway.

And you're going to remember all of it. But why?

You scramble through the fire safe, looking at everything that is fading, just in case it escapes you. You thumb through the wedding photos, run your fingers along the watermark on Tom's birth certificate, flip through page after page of data strains you made to help yourself remain sane.

The data strains.

They might have helped keep your memory intact.

True dialogic never hedge a rune.

The mailman creeps up the steps behind you. "Yo, Milton."

You turn, a pathetic huddled up mass of tears and Schauss pink poop stains running down your boxer briefs. "Hey."

The mailman recoils in shock. "Damn, man. You alright?"

"I'll be fine."

He hands you a stack of papers. "These were in your mailbox.

No postage. I can't send them like this."

"I—" You laugh through the tears. "Oh, shit. Yeah I forgot the stamps. You get a chance to read them?"

The mailman hands them to you, shakes his head. "I couldn't make heads nor tails of it. Word salad, man."

You open the first paper, expecting to see "My Love is a Tussin Vulture."

But it's exactly as the mailman says: word salad. "Thanks. I'll get some stamps and leave them in the box for tomorrow."

The mailman nods and heads back down the stairs. "Feel better, man."

"Will do."

You wait for him to close the downstairs door and drag the fire safe back inside, leaving the birth certificates and wedding photos on the step outside your door. Those fuckers aren't—can't—disappear again.

You unfold your love poems to the mailman on your counter: word salad.

You distinctly remember writing something about bubble wrap right here at the counter. But there's no mention of bubble wrap here.

In fact, there's no remnant of anything you recall writing about. What you see before you are data strains, vaccines. Were you trying to protect the mailman, even to the degree that you were deluding yourself about what you were writing?

You set the data strains down on the table and head for the birth certificates and wedding photos to find the wedding photos partially faded. They're overexposed, and you're the missing element.

You bring them through the threshold. They disappear.

You bring them back outside: still faded.

Whatever pocket of foreshadowing your apartment offers, the gap between its prediction and the actual moment the prediction transpires seems to be slimming. You hold the birth certificates tight to your chest. "Bob!" you scream.

You wait.

"Goddamn it, Bob! I need to talk to you!"

You feel appendages cradle your shoulders. "Shhhhhh."

Not Bob.

You turn to confront your visitor.

"No. No," it whispers. "Stay right where you are." You feel a proboscis slide up your back gently. "We told you to cheer up. Why didn't you listen?"

"My kids are going to disappear."

"Not if you just shut. It. Off."

"I can't."

"Then there's only one solution." The appendages release their grasp.

You turn.

Al Bundy dressed as a fly or a fly dressed as Al Bundy holds up a writhing larva. "This." He wiggles it gently. It writhes against his grasp. "Can solve our problem."

"I-I'm listening," you stutter.

"If you let her in, she can filter your excretions."

You swallow deeply. "In where? My mouth or my . . ."

"The latter of your suggestions would be optimal."

You slowly back toward the door. "You know, I'm feeling pretty decent, save that little epiphany about the birth certificates. I'll probably bounce back pretty quickly."

"We're trying to help."

"By sticking a giant maggot up my ass?" You step backwards through the door. "No thanks." You slam the door shut behind you and run down the stairs, birth certificates in hand.

You run for the bridge, equipped with your new mantra: *fuckfuckfuckfuckfuckfuck* until you see Beth getting gas with the kids at pump three, at which point your mantra escalates to *FUCKFUCK-FUCKFUCKFUCK!* Christ, does she *live* at the Sunoco now?

"Milton!" She waves you over. "Are you crying?"

"I'll be fine."

"You found them?"

You hand her the birth certificates. "In the fire safe, like I said."

"Throw them in with Tom, alright?" She nods to the back seat. "I ought to be back tomorrow night, maybe the night after. Depends on how Mom's feeling."

You open the rear passenger-side door and set the birth certificates on Tom's lap. "You kids be good for Mom, alright."

Tom looks up from his 3DS. "You look like shit, Dad."

Karen reaches for you. "Come with us, Daddy!"

"No can do, Karen." You reach in for a hug and pat Tom on the head as you exit the vehicle. "Daddy's got to get happy, kids."

Beth pumps the last few pennies of gas into the tank. "You sure this is the right time for that, Milton?"

You turn and smile at her.

"Put a fucking plug in the jug, ya drunk!"

FOURTEEN
DUELING PURGES

YOUR kids are going to disappear. Your marriage is already crumbling, but you'd rather it crumble than "never was."

You're fading out of your wedding pictures, and you're afraid this might mean you're going to disappear. You're afraid that you'll become never was.

You were conditioned at a young age in the Catholic Church. As such, fear begets thoughts of God.

You wonder if there's a place in heaven and purgatory for things that never were, and if we have souls, what happens to the souls of those who simply materialize as a result of chaos when they're sent back to wherever they came from?

Moreover, if you reach a point at which you no longer exist, what happens to all of the changes you made? Will everything you shit out of existence be restored, including yourself, your marriage, and your children? Are you just part of the cosmic ebb and flow of chaos and order, shitting yourself in and out of existence like some sort of broken Magic: The Gathering combo?

As you reach the bridge, you realize your mind is working overtime to devise a philosophy that will promote apathy. Your mind wants to return to its natural state. Things were so much easier when you were just jerking off in the dark after scotch taping clips from VHS tapes together. You wonder how much of your speculation about what is happening has been guided by your desire to return to your madness.

You realize that perhaps a good part of your madness occurred because you had too much time to think, because you haven't thought about data strains, verbal infections, or miasma longitudinal coronary in a long time.

You duck into the shadows beneath the overpass. Ghost Bob hovers near the grunge-era graffiti. He ghosts the tags.

"Bob."

He ghosts to you. "I was worried about you."

"Where have you been? I called to you earlier."

"I've been here."

"I don't think either of us are going to be for much longer."

"What do you mean?"

You hold up your wedding pictures. "These disappear in my apartment." You point to the faded image. "The process is already happening out here."

"I hope you didn't pay that photographer."

"These pictures were normal a few months ago. I looked at them after Beth left almost every day. Whatever is happening, it's making parts of my life disappear."

"I don't think it works like that. We're just changing small things, things most people don't even notice. We just have an eye for detail."

You shake your head. "Big shit is changing, Bob. Tang is back."

"What the fuck is Tang?"

"Some powdered drink or something. I don't know. Anyway, think about what something that seems small to us means. If an entire product disappears and reappears, that means factories are likely disappearing and reappearing too. Folks who work in their factories gain and lose jobs. Hell, some of them might not exist. They might disappear or reappear with the factory. Something as small as a single ingredient, there's got to be a factory that processes that ingredient for us in other products. What happens to all of that?"

"I don't know."

"Did any of you think this through?"

Ghost Bob just stares at you.

"Where's Dave?"

"Dave?"

"Yes, Dave. Tall fuck. Sniffs ass and bleeds into the burning barrel." You jog to the riverside. "I need to talk to him."

In the rising waters, Gary splashes that fucking bird. The bird raises its wings defensively, puffs up.

"Gary."

He turns to you. His smile fades.

"Where the fuck is Dave?"

He looks at Ghost Bob, ghosting down the hill behind you. "Who's Dave?"

"You've got to be kidding me."

Gary steps out of the water slowly, brows furrowed in confusion.

"There's no way. You guys are fucking with me. He'd be the last of us to go."

Ghost Bob ghosts your shoulder. "I know this has been hard on you, and you're right. Things are changing. Fast. But you're not going to disappear. None of us are going to disappear."

You shrug his ether-hand off your shoulder. "You can't say that with certainty. None of us know what's going to change. Dave led us down the rabbit hole with a few examples of shit that seemed off. Now things are more fucked than they ever were."

Gary opens his palms. "Who. The fuck. Is Dave?!"

"He's the one who got us into this! He's the first temperament. Blood."

"*You* got us into this, Milton!" Gary shouts. "You convinced me I was barfing the Berenstein Bears back to an 'ain' spelling, and it worked. I don't know if it was me that caused it, but it changed back to the way I remembered it. Now you're telling me that if we keep doing this we're going to shit and puke ourselves out of existence?"

"Berenstain Bears have always been 'ain'," Ghost Bob adds.

"That never happened, Gary. Why the fuck would I rope you

into this? You're trying to fuck my wife!"

"Maybe I've always been fucking your wife, Milton. Maybe the Mandela Effect just makes you think I haven't been."

Your stomach drops. "That how you remember it?" There's no point in debating this any further. Gary and Bob are infected. You had hoped at least Gary would have watched your data strain vaccines and perhaps that would have prevented this from happening. You weren't aggressive enough and now entire parts of reality are being wiped from collective memory via some thought transmitted order virus.

Gary pulls a bottle of ipecac syrup out of his shirt pocket. "You really think we can purge one another out of existence? Let's test that theory right now." He downs the bottle. "I'm going to puke you off the planet, you crazy cuck fucker."

A load of Schauss pink foam drops into your pants. The smell of hibiscus erupts from your nether region. "Go for it."

Gary drives his finger down his throat.

Ghost Bob holds his hand out. "Not yet! You'll throw up the ipecac!"

You shit again. "Why the fuck are you helping him?!"

Ghost Bob shrugs. "I'm not taking sides."

"It doesn't matter. It isn't like we control what happens around us. The balance shifts and things just disappear. You can't choose to puke until I disappear, Gary."

"I puked Berenstain Bears back into existence. I can puke you out."

Gary's sense of agency in all of this frightens you. In his memory, you taught him how to direct the expelled foam toward things he wanted to see change. But you have no recollection of this.

But maybe he's right. Maybe if you focus hard enough, you can control what goes.

The fear works in your favor. More of the foam billows from your bowels. You drop your pants and let it fall onto the earth below.

You have a head start.

You close your eyes and try to will Gary out of existence.

Gary punches himself in the stomach. "Come on! Work!"

You continue, hunched over the ground below you. Your legs grow tired as the foam builds beneath you. When your bowels reach capacity, the foam bubbles out of your ears.

Gary punches himself again. "It used to work faster than this."

Ghost Bob ghosts Gary's back. "You're putting too much pressure on yourself."

The foam begins to gather around your eyes. You squeeze your tear ducts and the air pockets squeal like a tiny mammal. "Will you stop helping him?!"

"Fuck this!" Gary lunges toward you, knocking you into your foam.

"What the fuck?"

"If I'm not going to barf, I'm going to drag your goofy ass to the concrete and pin you theeeraaaaalph!" Streams of pink foam rocket onto your face.

As you roll Gary onto his back and pin him, more foam dribbles from your ears. You're both slick with foam. You can't tell where Gary's foam ends and yours begins.

Gary turns his head and vomits again.

Ghost Bob grows erect.

You push yourself off Gary. "We need to stop!" You wipe the foam from your eyes. "Christ, I can't even see, it's so thick!"

Gary sits up and pulls the vial out of his pocket. "Can't. Ipecac, dumbass." He hurls onto his chest, soaking his shirt.

"We could both disappear! We need to control this."

Gary inhales sharp and deep, waiting for the next round. "I've been puking for weeks. I barely even use the ipecac anymore. I don't even eat anymore."

"You're going to kill yourself."

"I don't care." Gary looks up. "Does he have an erection?" He rises to his feet. "What the fuck, Bob?"

"I can't help it."

"You don't even have a body, Bob." You swat at the foam pouring from your ears. "Fucking ghost popping ether boners while we wrestle to the death."

Ghost Bob smiles. "You have to admit, it is kind of sexy."

Gary vomits again. "This is some Jerry Springer shit right here. You think we can make money off of it?"

"I think you'd end up in a nut house," Ghost Bob replies.

"Or as a government experiment," you add, laughing momentarily. "We're fucked." You buckle.

Ghost Bob ghosts to your side. "What's wrong?"

"Something big. Inside me."

"You okay?"

You nod. "I've been shitting out these egg things."

"Egg things?"

"People, places."

Gary stands over you. "Places?"

"The daycare by Super Center, that came out of me."

"Bullshit." Gary vomits again.

"You're going to see in a minute here." You feel your cheeks part. "Whatever it is, it's coming. Now."

Ghost Bob ghosts your hand. "You'll be alright."

Gary stands behind you. "My God!"

You crane your neck to take in the behemoth egg inching out of your anal cavity.

You feel Ghost Bob loosen his grasp. You look down at your hand. He's holding on just as tight as before, but he's fading, just like your image in the wedding photos. "Bob . . ."

Ghost Bob smiles. "You're doing the right thing."

Gary vomits.

Ghost Bob's ether boner deflates.

The fucking bird hops up to your egg, picks at it curiously with his beak.

Ghost Bob flickers in and out of existence.

The egg drops and cracks.

Gary pokes it. "What the fuck is in that thing?"

You roll over to look at it. "Open it up."

Gary leans over the egg. He places his hands in the crack. "It safe?"

"Yeah."

He tears it open. Steps back.

"What's in there?"

"A Super Center shift manager." He peers in.

You look inside. "It's Bob."

"Who?"

You correct yourself. "Ghost Bob."

"Who the fuck is Ghost Bob?"

You grab Gary by the shoulders. "He was just. Fucking. Here!" You let him go. "You seriously don't remember Dave, do you?"

Gary shakes his head.

"Goddamn it, Gary. We have to stop."

"We're so close," Gary says.

"You can't even tell what the world was like five minutes ago. How the fuck can you tell we're close to being the way things were?" *Moreover*, you think, *why can I remember?*

"I can feel it."

You feel it too.

No wait, that's just another contraction in your stomach. "Fuck. Another one's coming."

"If I shit you into one of those shift managers . . ." You claw at the ground, trying to ease the pain. "I'm sorry."

Shift Manager Bob steps out of his egg and begins wandering aimlessly at the river's edge.

The last thing you remember is your eyelids feeling heavy. They begin to close. Darkness encroaches. You think you're dying, then you realize your eyes are wide open. The black underbellies of swarming flies have canvassed the sun. They rush northeast, carrying briefcases and larvae, little flybabies in their arms.

You wake up the next morning, or what you assume is the following morning. It is daylight, and the sun is dancing on the eastern horizon. You know it is morning, but you're not sure which morning.

Something obscures your view. You blink the world into focus to find yourself surrounded by Super Center shift managers. They seem oblivious to your presence.

They stumble into one another, like perfume molecules in this entropy simulation you watched when you were young. Except the shift managers don't disperse. They just ricochet off one another around you. You get to your feet and count heads. There are at least twenty of them. You spot shift manager Bob. You shake him. "Bob!"

He does not respond.

You scan the faces to see if you recognize the others. You are particularly interested in seeing if you birthed a new incarnation of Gary.

He's nowhere to be found. Not real Gary. Not shift manager Gary.

You head for the roadway.

The shift managers follow.

You shoo them away. "Go!"

They cower from your gesture, but flock to you once your arms fall to your sides.

You wave them off again. "Come on, guys. Fuck off."

Slowly they lurch to your side like zombies.

"Fine." You turn. "Come on. I'll take you home."

"Home," one of the shift managers says.

"Home?" they all ask in near unison.

You walk the shift managers past the Polk High football field. You all climb the chain link fence near Super Center, wade waist deep into a small duck pond. You walk through the pond to the other side, and notice a family eating lunch at a picnic table. You notice they are staring at you. You notice a small dirt path from the picnic area to the Super Center. You notice you could have easily avoided the duck pond.

You notice you're a fucking idiot.

A tree at the edge of the parking lot rustles in the wind.

You pass it and enter the store.

The security panels scan you for ID.

The shift managers pull their IDs out of their pockets and follow you through the panels.

Then finally, when you get inside, they disperse.

They disperse to the bread aisle, and turn the labels on jars of Jiffy so the logos all face outward.

They disperse to the powdered drinks and adjust the Tang.

They head to the body soap section and adjust the Lava soap with yellow #2.

FUCK HAPPINESS

So not everything has changed.

You remember Beth. You remember Tommy and Karen, and you rush home, hoping they've survived the transition.

FIFTEEN
FUCK PURITY

YOU step into your apartment, your pocket of foreshadowing that has become almost wholly synonymous with the outside world.

Jiffy inside.

Jiffy outside.

You haul your fire safe to the doorstep.

Missing photos become faded photos.

You're still trapped in a failing marriage. You blink and the entire trajectory from the day you said "I do" to the day Beth said "fuck off" flashes before your eyes. Schauss pink relief washes over you, courses through your veins, and runs down the side of your face. Something broken is salvageable. Something that never was is impossible to recover unless you can shit it into existence at the cost of losing something else in an ad infinitum game of diminishing returns until nothing is left but absolute purity.

You wonder if memory—in all its broken, disordered splendor—can even exist in a world without chaos.

You realize memory—in all its broken, disordered splendor—essentially serves the same function as your randomized data strains.

Subjectivity is the vaccine to thought infections. Maybe.

Ignorance keeps you clean.

You drop the wedding photos back into the safe and check your answering machine. You've always found its arrhythmic blinking unsettling. It skips a beat and doubles up like the heart palpitations you used to get in undergrad. Has your answering machine been sneaking NoDoz out of the medicine cabinet, fighting off sleep for twenty-four hours just to let you know you have five new messages?

The first is from Beth: "Hey, we made it to Mom's. Give me a call when you get a chance."

The second is also from Beth: "Milton, where the fuck are you?"

Third: "What the fuck? Why do you insist on keeping this shitty landline if you never answer the phone?"

Fourth: "Mil"

Fifth: "Ton"

You pick up the phone and autodial the last incoming number.

"Milton?"

"Yeah. Sorry."

"Where were you?"

You catch your breath. "At the store."

"You had to work?"

"Um, yeah."

"You could have let me know."

"I got called in. It was last minute." You look at the fire safe. "Kids alright?"

"Karen's fine."

Your heart mimics the answering machine's light. "Tommy?"

"He's being a little shit. Forgot his charge cord. I'm trying to find one at Super Center."

"You probably won't have much luck."

"Yeah, well. Gotta try."

"You might be able to find one at Game Stop, or whatever equivalent they have down there."

"You think they'll have copies of the kids' birth certificates there?"

"What?"

"The fucking birth certificates, Milton. The sheets you gave us were blank."

"They weren't. Those were the birth certificates."

"Yeah, well. I'm sitting down here wondering if I should even interview. They said it shouldn't be a problem, but it still makes me look like I don't have my shit together."

"You need to come home."

"Look. I know you're worried about custody, but we're not getting back together. We'll sort out the details once I know what's going on with this job."

"I know we're not getting back together." But you don't know, and your hope hasn't fully died, even after her repeatedly telling you she's never coming back. "But you need to bring the kids back."

"We'll be home tomorrow." She jumps right into another line of conversation to deter pleading. "You know what I did find?"

"What's that?"

"Fucking Jiffy."

"It's on the shelves up here now too. You want to check on something else for me?"

"Sure."

"Check the dye in the Lava soap."

"Alright. Hang on a minute." You hear her tearing off a plastic bag in the produce aisle.

You breathe heavily into the phone, waiting for her to shuffle over to the toiletries. You try to make small talk. "Good drive down?"

"You know it sucks. It was quiet though."

"That's hard to believe with Karen."

"She had headphones. Alright. I've got the soap."

"Check the dye. Is it yellow #2 or yellow #5?"

"Yellow #5."

"It's still yellow #2 here."

"Maybe just different state regulations? California thinks everything causes cancer. Maybe New York isn't far behind?"

"I don't think so. It's #5 in my apartment, but #2 outside." You pause, trying to think of how to frame what you think is happening. "I'm pretty sure my apartment is prophetic or something. Like whatever is different in here becomes different outside a few days later. But I think the changes are migrating north slowly, like the flies."

"Flies?"

"The ones that were working at Super Center?"

"What the fuck are you talking about?"

"You don't remember?" She's infected. You should have made her watch your edit of *Country Cuzzins.* "There were flies. I saw them fly north yesterday. The important thing is that when the flies left, almost everything went back to the way it was in my apartment. Jiffy. The shift managers. There's some sort of correlation between those flies and the things that are changing. Either they move because things are changing or things change because they move."

"You realize that if I hadn't seen the Jiffy shit with my own eyes, I'd think you're fucking crazy right now."

"Well I'm glad you still remember that, because I need you to trust me when I tell you that you need to get the kids in the car and get home as soon as possible."

"I will be home tomorrow."

"Tomorrow might be too late. The birth certificates weren't in the fire safe in the apartment. They appeared when I moved the fire safe into the hallway. Same with our wedding pictures. I think the kids are in danger. I think they could disappear next. Drive north. Have Tommy keep an eye on the birth certificates. If the writing doesn't return by the time you get back, I'll give you full custody of the kids."

"You'd like that, wouldn't you? Just completely abandon all responsibility."

"Please. Listen to me. Come. Home. If I'm right about the flies, about everything changing, the kids should be okay if we head north until the birth certificates re-materialize."

"Are you crying?"

"It's that fucking foam shit." You wipe your eyes. "I just want the kids to be safe."

"Fuck me." She sighs. "Alright. I'll pack them up. But if you have those birth certificates I'm going to fucking kill you, Milton."

"You have the birth certificates. Have Tommy watch them as you drive. Let me know when and where the writing re-appears."

"Jesus Christ, Milton."

"So you'll do it?"

"I already said yes."

"Okay. I'll be home a little later. I'm heading north to see if I can catch up with the flies."

"I feel like I'm being sucked into some collective hysteria. Like none of this is actually real. It's just like your fucking thesis. Your madness is like a fucking black hole. It just sucks everything around it in."

"This is real, Beth."

"That's what all crazy fuckers say."

"Just come home. If I'm wrong, I'll admit myself to the psych ward. Whatever you want, I'll do it."

"Alright. I'll get the kids. On my way."

"Thank you."

"Yeah, yeah."

You stay on the line as Beth buckles herself into her car. You hear the engine come to life and the call ends.

You fish your wedding pictures out of the fire safe and toss the box back into your apartment. You close the door and head for PCK FCE.

You toss the faded wedding photos on the passenger seat and buckle in.

You glance over occasionally as you drive, waiting for your image to reappear in the photo of Beth.

You drive through rural town after rural town. Each is a facsimile of the previous: a post office, a playground, a town hall, and the same house designs side-by-side down Main Street. A minivan and a truck in every gravel driveway. Poor man's Americana.

This is the land of Jiffy. These are the houses Tang calls home.

You drive past A-frame houses with cheap wood paneling, past Dodge Grand Caravans, and kids playing basketball on cracked pavement ball courts.

The wedding photos do not change.

You drive past double-wide trailers and modular homes, past quaking aspen and rows of pine.

In the photos Beth's hair changes color. Her smile grows less pronounced, and your image phases in.

You drive past cauldrons or lakes or cauldrons and lakes. You drive past blue cicadas and mothmen.

In the image, you see your silhouette. Then your fingers crossed through Beth's.

You drive past mountains cradled by a razorwash backdrop, checkerboard pillars, and pools of liquid static.

You drive into the mouth of chaos and see bloated cattle dot the horizon.

The picture beside you has returned to normal, or at least to the way you remember it. You're not sure when, but you know it was somewhere between quaking aspen and the mothmen.

You watch black clouds of flies swarm just overhead, and you shudder, knowing that this will be your children's safe haven from the world outside these boundaries.

You search for Dave.

You search for CPS offices, or DSS buildings, of which there are none.

You search beneath rusted overpasses, near the shorelines of Jiffy rivers.

But Dave is nowhere to be found.

You drive back toward the minivans and modular homes until you reach the cauldron or lake or cauldron and lake.

Your image begins to fade from the picture on your passenger seat.

Chaos collides with order here, with only a slim liminal space between the two. This small space is a bridge between two worlds, the bridge between chaos and order.

You park your car and follow the space between the world you knew and the world you know, the space between Jif and Jiffy.

And you find him perched on the lowest branch of an application tree on the edge of chaos. "We're so close."

"You lied to me."

"About what?"

"My wife, my kids. Everything important to me will be gone if we keep going. You told me I was being paranoid."

"In the grand scheme of things, it is a small price to pay."

"You don't get to decide the value of the things I love."

"The things you love never were, Milton."

"They're here now."

"You won't remember them once they're gone. You won't remember any of this. You don't remember half of the things you've already lost. Your memory holds on better than most, but it won't last forever. Eventually you'll have forgotten all of it. But all things considered even that doesn't matter."

"Why?"

"Because you'll be gone too. All of this will be gone." He drops from the branch and walks toward you. "I tried to find an easier way. I really did. But whoever or whatever created me made me flawed.

"I created all of you miserable bastards, little living, breathing soulboxes so I could store bits of myself away, hoping you'd cultivate me into a perfect being once I harvested all of you. But you were all flawed too. For every person who led a spiritual life, another would fall into hedonistic trappings. I'd reap one pure soul and one impure soul, and everything would balance out.

"Then I tried the whole messiah thing. Invested just about every drop of yang into a single person. I planned on letting him roam the planet while I filled the newborns with yin until I was just about depleted. Once my ether was exhausted I planned on sacrificing the messiah so I'd be composed of yang exclusively. I had hoped that'd give me a chance to figure out how to rid the world of yin altogether . . . and they killed him about ten years before he was supposed to die." He waves his hands. "Free will and all . . . Third time's a charm though, right? Step-by-step we're going to peel away the layers of chaos and impurity until nothing remains."

You clench your fists. Foam begins to froth from your pores. You focus, and the foam stops. "I'm not helping you anymore."

"I noticed. You finally found purpose, and so you're happy now. But I don't need you to help me. I just need you to forget me. I can find more followers."

You turn toward the chaos to find yourself trapped in the liminal space.

"And you're not going anywhere until you do."

You panic and feel your insides knot up. *Don't shit. Don't shit. Don't shit.*

"This is even better than I'd imagined. You're not only going to forget. You're going to defecate until you forget. Maybe you'll tip the scales and get to see everything you love disappear before we're all wiped away."

Think. Think. You're trapped. You need to escape. You need to keep the foam at bay.

You collect yourself. Even if you can't escape, Beth is heading north. When she sees the writing on the birth certificates reappear, she'll know you were right. She'll follow you north. The kids will be safe.

Your bowels stop roiling. The world will go on without you.

You resign yourself to the fact that this is all beyond your control.

Dave shakes your shoulders. "What are you doing!?"

"I'm conceding. You win."

"Your kids are going to disappear. Why aren't you sad?"

You don't respond.

"Everything you know and love is going to die!"

You sit calmly, ignoring him.

"Shit, damn you!"

But you do not shit. Instead, you think of Beth driving your face into her pubic bone. You think of her naked in the shower. You grow erect and run your hand against your crotch.

You unzip yourself.

You tune Dave out and begin masturbating. You feel the tension in your body rise and fall arrhythmically, like the answering machine. Like your heart at the thought of loss.

You are the answering machine. You beep loudly so Beth can leave a message.

The beep sustains as you transition through multiple settings, your monotone alarm clock, the emergency test tone on an old analog television, the blood pressure machine at the local pharmacy.

Dave marches toward you, tries to shake you out of your masturbatory meditative state.

You whisper to yourself in data strain. The bluebird weeps placation in the forest fire night sweeps. Holy cortex and space-time diaspora.

You release your grasp on the conscious mind, on your agenda. You're searching for that Event Horizon moment, that spank-induced segue to escape.

You let go and trust in the mind as a self-regulating machine always veering toward self-flagellation. Maybe that's not everybody. Maybe that's just the Catholic in you. But it's your escape. The key to getting out of this place is shame and misery, and you have to walk the line between ejaculation and defecation to return home.

You climax, and some part of your brain fires, warning you to stop masturbating at the local pharmacy. But instead of shutting that part of the brain down by reminding it you're not in the pharmacy, you embrace it. *Yes*, you think. *I'm in the pharmacy. Naked. In the middle of the day. Masturbating furiously to the thought of my wife.*

Dave's voice grows distant as he continues shaking you. "Shit, goddamn it!"

His pleas are replaced by gentle organ music. The blood pressure machine tightens on your arm.

Your reading is 178/90

You're in the hypertension range.

You're also naked at the local pharmacy.

Pharmacy techs stumble into one another.

Nobody seems to notice you.

The machine releases its grasp and you run for the exit.

You run through the electric doors and toward the Giga Video.

You're free!

You're fucking free!

You're . . . struck down by a car in the middle of the road. You turn as the horn blares, in time to see Gary smiling as he mows you down.

SIXTEEN
FUCK GOODBYES

YOU wake up in complete darkness. You're in the pharmacy. You know this because the blood pressure cuff is wrapped tightly around your arm.

Around both arms.

Wait . . .

You're not in the pharmacy.

You tug at the blood pressure cuffs.

. . . These are not blood pressure cuffs.

"Squak!"

. . . That fucking bird.

"What the fuck, bird?"

"Squak!"

"Where am I? Turn on the fucking light."

The fucking bird flutters across the room and thrusts the light switch upward with his beak.

You're in your room.

"Can you unfasten me?"

The bird pokes you in the belly.

"So that's a no?"

The bird pokes you again.

"Look. I'm all cripped up anyway thanks to Gary. Let me at

least see if I'm capable of walking."

The bird just stares at you, head cocked.

"There's a bottle of Robitussin in it for you."

The bird pokes at you again, this time repeatedly.

"I'm serious. I bought it when Gary and I were supposed to take turns watching you."

"Squak!"

"I'm not telling you where it is. Untie me."

"Squak!" The bird tears at your belly button with its beak.

"Shit!" You flail. "Come on. Just get me out of this and I'll give it to you."

The bird just stares.

You lock eyes with him as you slide your arm up the bedpost as subtly as possible.

This isn't your first time locked and left like this.

One arm free.

You reach over to your other arm and push the knot up over the opposite post.

You sit up. "Alright, bird. Let's get you that Robitussin." You hold out your arm.

The stupid fucking bird hops right up onto your wrist.

You stand.

It unfurls its wings to regain balance.

You smile.

The bird smiles.

You ring the fucking bird's neck.

The bird chokes. Pink foam runs down the corner of its mouth.

Your grip tightens. No foam. Not today.

The bird flaps wildly and begins pecking at your fingers. It jabs at your knuckles until it breaks skin.

You let go.

You're not strong enough to take a life, not even a bird's life.

Ed hops to the window and flies toward the Giga Video, toward Giga Video Gary.

You head for the stairs.

You notice the answering machine blinking on the way out.

One message.

Beth.

"Hey, Milton. Should be home shortly. We're stopping to eat real quick at Arby's in Gouverneur."

You check the digital clock on the machine. It blinks 1:42. It hasn't been set since you've owned it.

You hobble to the Giga Video. Gary's car—now emblazoned in your mind—sits in the parking lot near the propane tanks. If you had a gun, you could blow the entire store sky high from your bedroom window.

You feel guilty for even imagining the scenario, in part because hurting innocent people strikes you as wrong, in part because you imagine aiming for the propane tanks beneath a new curtain rod, which you still haven't fucking purchased.

You really do need to get that curtain rod.

But right now, you need to talk to Gary.

You walk through the front doors and Gary is behind the counter, processing new releases.

"Hey, fucker!" you shout.

He looks up. "Hey, man." He tries to smile disarmingly. "You okay?"

"I suppose, considering you hit me with a car and then tied me up in my fucking bedroom. What the fuck, by the way?!"

"I needed to finish up my shift. I left Ed to watch over you."

"This needs to stop, Gary. Look at us. Look at everything around us. This is the byproduct of our purging." You point to the lottery ticket dispenser, the iced tea coolers, and the display racks of Little Debbie snacks. "It's all so mundane."

"I happen to like Little Debbie."

"Maybe that's the next thing to go."

"Doubtful."

"That seems to be the end result. Think about it, what we're doing is systematically whitewashing the world. The flies are gone. Where's Polk High? The mountains near Super Center. It's all gone."

"What the fuck are you talking about?"

"Did Dave put you up to this?"

Gary stares intently at the counter. "Dave?"

As he leans down you see a small vial of ipecac syrup in his shirt pocket. You grab him by the collar and smash the vial against his chest. "Don't bullshit me, Gary! I almost bought your act under the bridge, but you watched those data strains I returned to Giga-Video. You're immune to the order virus just like me. You remember everything!"

Gary tears away from you, starts lapping at the ipecac on his shirt. "You fucking nut bag. I'm going to vomit you to oblivion—"

You grab him again and jump onto the counter. You tear from the collar of his shirt downward. Plastic buttons fly across the floor.

Gary struggles against you, but you easily pin him to the floor. You're stronger than you remembered. Your Jif biceps are now Jiffy biceps.

You choke Gary out with your Jiffy biceps.

You watch his face redden. He white knuckles your wrists, but cannot pull you off. You can feel the life leaving him.

Then that fucking bird flies out of the back room, wings spread. He sinks his claws into your head and the back of your neck.

Gary gasps for air as you grab Ed by his legs. You pull the bird down over your head and slam him into Gary's face repeatedly.

Gary throws oxygen-starved punches that barely make their target.

You push the bird into his face and he begins slapping at you.

The fucking bird rattles against your hands and Gary's face.

You keep pressing until their motions transition from sluggish to weak and spasmodic.

The bird stops moving, and you keep pushing it into Gary's mouth. You remember your wife doing the same to you with her bush, wonder if she's done the same to Gary, and you push the dead bird harder into Gary's face.

Gary stops struggling.

You drop the bird on the floor next to Gary.

Someone comes through the front door. "Is anyone here?"

Fucking Beth?!

She walks closer to the counter. "Gary?"

She sighs and marches out.

You search under the counter for something to restrain Gary, settle on a few bungee cords that you use to hogtie him up.

You drag him into the break room and tuck him under the manager's desk.

Now what?

You need those data strains.

You scour behind the counter for the films. You edited three in total. *Country Cuzzins*, *Blood Feast*, and *The Greasy Strangler*.

The hard shells are coded by number, so you run to the cult section and get the numbers:

Country Cuzzins: 1517

Blood Feast: 1502

The Greasy Strangler: 1543

You run back to the counter and find the movies, turning periodically to make sure Beth doesn't see you.

1517 is checked out.

1502 and 1543 are on the shelves.

You grab them and peer over the counter, waiting for Beth to leave.

You watch her drive down the road and pull into your driveway.

You hobble to catch her.

You see her helping Karen out of the back seat.

Tommy's not there.

Answering machine arrhythmia. "Where's Tommy!?"

Beth sets Karen down. "He went in to see you."

"Does he have the birth certificates?"

She rounds the car and pulls them out of his booster seat. "The text reappeared around Jamestown, I think. Tommy wasn't watching closely."

"That's fine." You head for the stairs. "We have to go."

"Where?"

You turn at the door. "North."

As you reach the stairs, Tommy is already opening the door and stepping through. "No!"

Tommy steps through the threshold.

You reach the top of the stairs.

Tommy turns to you. "What's wrong?"

"Nothing." You reach in for him. "We have to go."

You step over the threshold. You're in a cauldron or lake or cauldron and lake. You hear the drone of chamber flies. In every direction, thousands of you refracted in black, broken-mirror eyes.

You step back.

You're back at the threshold to your apartment.

Tommy stares, mouth agape.

"What just happened?" You clarify, "What did you see?"

"You disappeared. Completely."

"Let's get you in the car. Do you have anything here you need?"

Tommy runs for the couch. "My charge cord."

"Hurry up."

You follow Tommy down to the car.

You run your hand through his hair. "Getting shaggy," you say, so he isn't so unnerved by the fact that you're touching him. Then you hug him.

"What's going on, Dad?"

You hold him tight. "Not sure, but you'll be safe if you keep going north."

You walk to Karen's door, give her a hug. "You be good for Mommy, okay?"

"Aren't you coming with us?"

"I'll catch up with you in a few days," you say. "I have a few things to take care of here." You close her door and wave Beth into the apartment. "I need to talk to you for a minute." You take her hand and lead her to the top of the stairs. "They're going to be okay. Tommy walked through the door. He was fine." You open the door. "I just need you to step across."

She tries to break away from your grasp.

"Don't." You hold her hand tighter. "If you disappear I want to be able to pull you back through."

She steps through the doorway and becomes the woman you married. Her blond hair is pushed back, pinned on one side with a barrette that skirts style lines between flapper and junior. "I'm fine," she smiles. "Idiot."

"You know I still love you, right?"

"I know." She looks around the living area. "I'm going to miss this place."

You look at her longingly.

She rolls her eyes. "Look, I love you too, alright. Just not the way I used to."

"But you did love me, once?"

"Yes, stupid. I married you, didn't I?"

"I suppose you did." On some level you had hoped she still loved you. You had hoped that walking through that threshold would foreshadow her return to a time when she loved the man who forgot to fix the curtain rod, who forgot to buy the kids vitamins. You had hoped that order might have stripped away the chaos that led her to leave you. "Why did you leave?"

"You just—you gave up, Milton. Not just on us. On everything. You dove wholly into that stupid thesis."

"My head was always in the clouds though. I was always disengaged. It never bothered you before."

"It never bothered me because it never affected me. But towards the end it was . . . infectious. I started giving up too. Then that shit you were writing, I used to look at it sometimes, just to gauge how crazy you were going. It started to make sense. Like I knew it was convoluted, but I could still understand it." She looks down.

You follow her eyes, see she notices your hand gone from the wrist down. She pulls away. Your arm falls to your side outside the threshold and your hand reappears.

Even if she did still love you on that side of the door, you wouldn't be able to touch her.

And you can't decide which reality would be crueler.

"You'll take the kids north then?"

She nods. "How far?"

"Until you see the flies. They'll guide you home."

"Flies?"

"Just remember, okay? Follow the flies."

"Okay."

"You'll want this." You hand her the copy of *Blood Feast*. "When you get there, watch the last fifteen minutes of the movie."

"A bit gory for the kids, don't you think?"

"I edited it. It's a vaccine. It'll help you all remember, in case something happens."

She takes the video. "We're not going to see you again, are we?"

You shake your head. "I don't think so."

"You never did replace that curtain rod."

"I know. I'm sorry."

"I'm sorry too. Bye, Milton."

"Goodbye, Beth."

She walks out of the porch. You hear her car door slam, and she pulls out of the driveway. You wait to hear her car hit the lip at the end of the driveway and pull away.

You reach your hand across the threshold.

It disappears.

You pull it back through.

You have to do this. You can't risk defecation.

You grab the doorknob and step over the threshold, closing the door behind you.

Al Bundy masquerading as a fly or a fly masquerading as Al Bundy waits for you in the darkness.

"I think this is the answer you're looking for." You hand him your copy of *The Greasy Strangler*. "Make them dream in data strain," you say.

Al Bundy masquerading as a fly or a fly masquerading as Al Bundy nods. "Wads of God's dirty digits all gathered round," he mutters.

"Piloted through the nightscape veil-lifted," you reply.

ÉPILOGUE

BETH, Karen, and Tom walk to the Super Center. They walk past the Polk High football field. They climb the chain link fence near Super Center, wade waist deep into the cauldron or lake or cauldron and lake. They walk through the bottom of the lake to the other side, over divots in the mountain ranges. Micro-valleys.

Once they get past that first row of security panels, the kids dart away from Beth toward the seasonal aisles in the front. Beth lingers on the clothes and magazines, watching the children from the corner of her eye.

She takes them to the toy section, lets her son's plastic pro wrestlers chase cardboard-encased supermodel facsimiles up and down the aisles. Karen comes at Beth with a pool noodle.

Tommy follows.

Your children beat at her ankles with discount pool noodles. Winter is almost here. It reminds her of the first time she was truly happy. But she can't remember why.

"Drops the dither façade down the stairs halted up over the rusted scraps?" they ask.

"Emerald shingles puppeteer the clouds, commanding a dark deposit," she replies.

The three flight moon dust and the head. First escaping the dark sparkle, that halved olive green of her eye. You want to be a part of it. To dip down into the manifolds of the whole. Trickling down the throat like a light rain.

The anchor. Somewhere highway lights splitting seams, piercing dreams, turn mountainside. A flux of crimson grates the air and earth, deafening the horizon. To behold dalliance.

Everything is as it always was, but Beth can't help but feel something is missing.

Something has always felt like it was missing . . . she thinks.

As the brisk kiss of winter cascades across her face through a hole in the Super Center ceiling, she remembers the peanut butter.

She plucks a jar of Jiffy from the shelves and throws it into her cart.

Nothing is missing.

Everything is as it always was.

There are many people without whom *Fuck Happiness* might never have seen the light of day. My wife, Amanda, and my daughters, whose independence gave me the time to write this book. Kevin Donihe, a voice of encouragement, support, and most important, reason. Shamus McCarty, Erika Instead, and Danger Slater, and Shane Cartledge, whose encouragement kept me moving forward when I was ready to throw in the towel. Ken Wood of *Shock Totem*, whose encouragement helped me not only develop a sense of autonomy as an author, but helped me work through subsequent novels. I ran on the fuel from that acceptance letter for a year and a half, man! It means more than you'll ever know. Finally, a huge thank you to Andersen Prunty and C.V. Hunt, who took me under their wing and helped restore my love of writing and publishing.

Kirk Jones (k3rk Dʒoʊnz): 1. English Director of *Nanny McPhee* 2. "Sticky Fingaz," rap artist and actor who played Blade for the television series 3. Canadian who survived a dive over Niagara Falls . . . only to return and pass upon his second attempt 4. Boring white author of *Uncle Sam's Carnival of Copulating Inanimals* (Eraserhead Press, 2010), *Journey to Abortosphere* (Rooster Republic, 2014), and *Die Empty* (Atlatl, 2017) who often gets mistaken for the other, arguably more notable, Kirk Jones fellows 5. Also not Kirk Byron Jones.

Other **Atlatl Press** Books